OOPS! I VOODOOED AGAIN

A MALVEAUX CURSE MYSTERY (BOOK 3)

G.A. CHASE

BAYOU MOON PRESS, LLC

Copyright © 2017 by G.A. Chase

First Edition 2017

Cover Art by Janet Holmes

Editing by Red Adept

ISBN eBook: 978-1-940299-43-3

ISBN Print: 978-1-940299-44-0

This book is a work of fiction. Names, characters, places, and incidents are products of the author's imagination or are used fictitiously. Any resemblance to actual events, locals, business establishments, or persons, living or dead, are entirely coincidental.

Bayou Moon Press, LLC

ABOUT THIS BOOK

Every time Kendell Summer thinks she has finally apprehended her ancestor, Baron Malveaux, the dastardly spirit slips from her grasp. His being freed from the voodoo totem to rejoin the living creates unprecedented dangers—too many for Kendell to face alone, causing her to turn to her newly discovered Wiccan counterpart, Sanguine Delarosa, for help.

Sanguine, however, comes with her own challenges. Acting more like a bratty younger sister than an accomplished swamp witch, Sanguine has her own secret agenda. And once again Kendell, her boyfriend, and her faithful pooch, Cheesecake, end up in harm's way while fighting for humanity's greater good.

But Sanguine is the key—if there is any hope of preventing a war between the living and the dead, Kendell and Sanguine must find a way to trust each other and work together.

"*C*an you help me?" a woman asked, out in the bar.

Myles cringed, having supposed the place empty. *Damnit, Charlie, you left the front door unlocked again.* As he looked up, he instantly forgot about the dripping dishrag in his hand. Blood was flowing from a three-inch gash in the woman's forehead into her left eye and down the side of her face. Her torn dress was so saturated with blood he couldn't tell what color it had been.

"I'll call 9-1-1," he said.

"Don't bother."

Her ripped blouse fell open as she walked to the bar. In the yellow glow of the blown-glass droplights that glamoured up the establishment, he saw her wounds weren't limited to her head. Where the soft curve of her cleavage should have been, flesh peeled away from her ribs. She sat on a barstool like any other customer.

The combination of water, alcohol, and sweat ran from

the rag down his arm like condensation from the night's humidity. He tossed the disgusting piece of terry cloth into the cleaning bucket. In spite of her wounds, he didn't see any blood where she'd walked. She had to be a spirit who'd succumbed to her injuries. He'd experienced dead souls in the voodoo realm of Guinee during his psychometric trances, but never while fully awake.

"How did you find me?" he asked.

"You're the only person whom I can see clearly. I don't even know how long I've been wandering the streets, but the longer I'm in this state, the more ethereal people seem."

"Do you know what happened to you?"

If a stabbing had happened recently in the French Quarter, the police would be asking questions. Myles wasn't a fan of being interrogated by cops with limited imaginations, but if the recently deceased were going to start wandering the streets, the loas of the dead wouldn't be far behind. If a member from either version of authority stopped by the bar, he needed to be prepared.

"That should matter to me, right—who killed me and why? I'm finding it hard to keep a handle on the facts regarding my life."

Myles still found the realm of consciousness released from life confusing though he'd been dabbling with it all his life. "I suspect dying is like being born. An infant doesn't give a lot of thought to the dramas of being in the womb. Do you have any connection to your body?"

She pulled the sides of her blouse together to hide the gashes. "You mean, when and where did I leave life's stage? I don't have a sense of time, but I've been wandering long enough to know that feeling of urgency is gone. The panic I felt at the end wasn't my final living emotion. There was a sense of being taken care of, like in a hospital. What's going to happen to me?"

Her explanation relieved his worry about the police. If she'd died in a hospital, they wouldn't be going bar to bar, looking for clues. However, the voodoo loas had misplaced a soul, and that was never good for the living or the dead, and especially not for Myles.

"I've only visited the *deep waters* for short periods of time. When I'm there, I find it hard to leave. You'll be a part of every other human soul, and they'll be a part of you. Eventually, you'll be like a cup of water floating in the ocean without the cup."

She hugged her stomach tighter. "What if I haven't been very good to people?"

In all of his mental journeys, he'd never experienced anything resembling judgement, only acceptance. "You have every bit as much right to join with others as anyone else. In life, we call the state of existence being loved, but once you pass through Guinee, it's the only reality that remains."

She looked up at his eyes. "But there is a place where I'll be judged?"

"You have to pass through the seven gates on your own. The loas who stand guard will ask you questions about what you've learned in life. Don't think of it so much as an interrogation as them trying to distill answers we all seek."

"How do you know so much about what happens after death?"

The memories of being possessed by the baron

Malveaux—who thought himself to be Baron Samedi, loa of the seventh gate of Guinee—continued to haunt Myles's dreams. "I was trapped in the afterlife for a time. My friends needed to move heaven and earth to free me."

She cowered away from the bar. "You spent time in hell?"

"Sorry, poor choice of phrases. It wasn't the place that was the problem. The loas of the dead were actually very nice to me. Guinee is more like purgatory. It's a chance to say goodbye to your life before letting go of everything that you were. The *deep waters*—which is where you go after Guinee—is neither heaven nor hell. Remove everything you know about your life, and exist as pure consciousness, and you'll find you're connected to every other being. It's the ultimate freedom."

She looked past him to the wall of bottles. "I'm going to miss drinking. Even though it might be a waste, could you pour me a shot of rum? I'd just like that one last memory of the booze flowing out of the bottle."

Charlie had already done the nightly inventory sheet before leaving, but one shot wouldn't be missed. As Myles poured the amber liquid into the miniature glass, he lifted the bottle to give the alcohol room to breathe. The heady smell was a nice change from the cleaning solvents.

"Drink it for me. Obviously, I can't pay you for it, but consider it my offering for your assistance."

He downed the shot, and its warmth spread to all parts of his body like the feeling of being appreciated. "The first gate isn't far. I can walk you there if you'd like. Wandering the streets of the Quarter alone at night is never a good idea, even for the dead."

"You're very kind. Maybe if my boyfriend had been more like you, I wouldn't be in this mess."

The bar was sufficiently clean for a Wednesday night. Myles made one last check to make sure no other beings were passed out in the bathrooms. Before leaving the bar, he sneaked a small bottle of rum into his back pocket.

They walked in silence for the first couple of blocks. Escorting a woman, even a dead one, in such a damaged state made him keep an eye on her—not that he could have done anything. Passing from the brightly lit area of Bourbon Street to the shadows of the Quarter put him on his guard.

She didn't seem to notice his discomfort. "Are there others like you who can see the dead?"

Looking as though he was talking to himself had the benefit of discouraging any potential thug, especially if the explanation was that he was talking to a dead woman and escorting her to a cemetery.

"If there are," he said, "they haven't confided their ability to me."

Her big blue eyes must have been quite captivating in life. With blood dripping into them, however, he found it hard to focus on her for long.

"And have you told anyone about your special abilities?" she asked. "People don't often give trust without first being trusted."

"There are a handful of people who know about my special brand of insanity."

She tried to kick him, but her foot just passed through his leg. "I'll bet your self-deprecation doesn't get you many girls. We like guys with confidence even if—especially if—their stories sound unbelievable at first."

"I've got a girlfriend who knows the truth. That's enough for me."

Saint Louis Cemetery No. 1 was creepy enough during the day, but the city-block-sized walled-in compound wasn't what was giving him the shakes. The neighboring housing project, which had replaced the elegant whorehouses of the Storyville era one hundred years before, made him wonder if his chivalry had been such a good idea. He longed for the bygone era. Being accosted by prostitutes selling their services had to beat being held up at knifepoint any night.

Myles approached the wrought-iron gates. As a prisoner of Baron Malveaux, he'd spent time on the other side, but the land of the dead wasn't meant for the living. He pulled out the bottle of rum and poured an offering to the loa of the dead.

Baron La Croix strolled out from between the tombs. "It's good to see you again, my friend."

Myles just wanted to drop the woman off and get back to his apartment. "I seem to have found one of your lost souls."

~

KENDELL SAT on the floor of her bedroom with Cecile—her whitewood acoustic guitar—in her lap. The problem wasn't the instrument but the pick she was twirling between her fingers like a half-dollar coin.

"I can do this without destroying another set of strings," she said.

Cheesecake, her somewhat overweight Lhasa apso, looked unconvinced as she lay on the bed, watching from her elevated position. Kendell typically received a constant low-pitched growl from her pup when using the dark powers for her music, but the guitar pick wasn't cursed. As a gift from Papa Ghede and the other loas of the dead, the token of appreciation wasn't meant to do any harm, not that the difference mattered to the pup. Anything magical made the old dog growl in disapproval.

"I promised to listen to you, and I am," Kendell said. "You were right about my work with Madam de Galpion causing Myles's problems, but you can't watch over me every minute. Isn't it better if I learn the limits of what I can do here with you than up on stage?"

The dog put her head on her paws as if to say, *We'll see.*

The late-afternoon light from the floor-to-ceiling window, which could open to a balcony over Decatur Street, reflected off the solid-gold pick. Learning music was never a challenge for Kendell, and trying to imitate a guitar legend's technique only proved useful to her in an academic sense. She was tired of paying homage to the greats. As Olympia Stain, lead guitarist for Polly Urethane and the Strippers, she would always be playing blues standards in the band's punk-rock style, but as Kendell Summer, she needed to break out of the mold she'd created.

The gold guitar pick was like a puzzle box with the

answer inside. All she had to do was figure out how to unlock its powers.

She looked back into Cheesecake's trusting eyes. "Every butterfly has to break out of her cocoon someday."

She leaned over the guitar and did her best to keep her mind from butting in. When it came to playing with raw emotion, she felt a kinship with only one musician, and playing his music might work as a transition from the known to the unknown.

"Computer, play 'Kind Hearted Woman Blues' by Robert Johnson."

Her fingers took up the challenge of playing both lead and rhythm guitar at the same time, but she left the singing to the digitized copy of the scratchy, worn, eighty-year-old recording emanating from her laptop.

Tears filled her eyes as the heart-wrenching emotions captured by the recording rolled over her. The magic wasn't in the chords or the words or even the technique. Like Myles's ability to detect strong emotions that had been left behind in objects, the voice of the bluesman carried a pain that could be felt but not understood. She'd done her best to copy his playing, but even if she managed an exact rendition, it would only be like a computerized copy of the Mona Lisa. The hand of the master was missing.

Cheesecake continued to stare at her, but at least the pup wasn't growling, as she had when Kendell had worked with the baron Malveaux's cursed items.

"This isn't going to be so easy, girl. I can see the mountain of learning ahead of me. This golden pick isn't a magic wand to get what I want but a means of seeing how far I have to go."

Kendell wondered if that was the difference between a gift from the devil versus one from a god. The devil would give a person what they wanted while a god would simply point the way.

"What was it Myles said? Success is earned, not given? I hate it when he's right. Don't tell him I admitted it."

Cheesecake would always keep her secrets.

As if mentioning his name had been enough to summon her boyfriend, Kendell heard the key in the lock. Quickly, she stashed the golden pick in her guitar case and got to her feet. She hadn't done anything wrong, but meddling with voodoo still made her feel guilty. *Time to remedy that.*

He looked tired and not simply in the way he often did after working too many long shifts without a day off. Their kiss was sweet but brief.

"I didn't know you were coming over," she said.

"I had a weird experience after work last night. At first, I wasn't going to tell you, but the more I thought about it, the worse I felt."

"I know what you mean." She was tempted to hide her attraction to voodoo from him. Her dabbling with the dark arts in the past had contributed to his possession by the baron, but like discovering music, it was a natural skill she couldn't ignore.

He sat next to Cheesecake on the bed and started scratching her ear—not the first time the pup had proven an emotional mediator. "My trips into human consciousness have opened a door. It's not like the one the baron passed through. No one's escaping from the other side, but apparently, the recently departed see me as some kind of guide to Guinee."

Kendell used the excuse of putting her guitar back into its case to grab the magical pick and hide it in her hand. Sitting on the other side of Cheesecake, she kept the golden triangle in her lap. "So we can expect ghosts to just walk in on us day or night? What do the loas expect? That you'll just take up the individual mysteries of how these people died?"

"I only briefly saw Baron La Croix. So far, I don't know what they want from me. It was just the one woman, but I thought you ought to know. There's something else. When I first met Baron Malveaux, he insinuated that I was a loa of the dead. I didn't believe him, but with this latest development, I'm thinking I need some answers."

She hadn't been on a lot of spiritual trips with Myles, but she knew the dangers. "I nearly lost you to the other side, and not just because of the baron. If I hadn't been there to pull you out of Guinee, would you have returned on your own?"

He stared into her eyes, revealing the conflict inside him. "I don't think I would have. It's not that I don't love this life, but hanging out with the loas was pretty enlightening, and continuing on to the *deep waters* has been a temptation I've had to resist all my life."

She stopped petting Cheesecake and took his hand. "You're not ready to go back. That bastard took more than just your strength." She took the guitar pick off her lap. "And I understand your temptation. This was a gift. I'm not sure how to use it, but it's not just some keepsake I can leave on my dresser."

He lifted her hand and kissed it. "I guess the afterlife isn't done with either of us."

~

MYLES HAD NEVER QUITE GOTTEN USED to sleeping in Kendell's bed. Between the seemingly endless number of pillows, the billowy comforter—which she insisted went with the décor, no matter the temperature—and Cheesecake, who always managed to take up half the bed, he felt like a dirty sock that had gotten lost in the sheets.

With the lights from the late-night music clubs on Decatur Street below her balcony, the room was never really dark. He eased out of the covers, trying not to wake the dog. She'd grown used to his presence in her mistress's bed, but that didn't stop her from following Myles around the apartment. After all Kendell had been through, he appreciated Cheesecake's constant vigil—just not when he desired a little solitude.

He pulled open the double-hung window that provided access to the outdoor veranda. Flowerpots overflowing with night jasmine hung from the cast-iron latticework and filled the air with a fragrance reminiscent of the Old South. He eased down into the chaise lounge to enjoy the music floating up from the jazz club a block away. The outdoor oasis was his favorite part of her apartment, particularly at night.

He jerked up in his chair at hearing her step onto the balcony. "I didn't mean to wake you."

She pulled her blanket up around her shoulders. "I always know when you get out of bed. Most of the time, I pretend to stay asleep so you can have your personal time, but I thought tonight you could use some company." The blanket covered the matching chair as she sat next to him.

"You must be the only person who gets cold on a summer night in New Orleans."

She hugged the blanket close. "Only after a gig with the girls. I'm so energized while I play I think my metabolism goes into overdrive. Then when I stop, my body gets very calm."

"I noticed. The same thing happens to you after we have sex."

She rolled onto her side to face him. "We need to talk about that."

He'd avoided the topic long enough. "I should have known you'd detect the change. Making love to you is still magical. I don't ever want you to think I'm not into it."

Her smile never failed to make him feel connected to her. "I know. But you have been more distant. And I know you come out here every night after we make love. What do you do out here?"

He lay back and looked at the stars over the river. "Just a quick check of my psyche."

"You're still afraid I might be infecting your spirit with the baron's soul? What's left of him is secure in Delphine's voodoo totem. I'd sacrifice my life before I saw you possessed by an evil spirit again."

Having Madam de Galpion in charge of the baron's soul hardly eased Myles's fears. He trusted her only slightly more than the man who'd been the impetus of the curse.

"I don't blame you," he said, "and I don't think you're filling me with some dark energy again. It's not that. Our souls meld together during sex. Two people becoming one always sounded like wedding-vow bullshit to me. Not any longer. It's not the sex, though. We'd already joined our spirits during our shared psychometric experiences. Sometimes, I just need to remind myself that I'm still a fully-functioning individual."

She reached across and held his hand. "I understand. We each still need our space. Sex with you isn't like anything I've ever experienced before. I know that's because we took that journey with our souls. I always thought being in a romantic relationship was as close as two people could be, but our partnership in investigating the curse, figuring out your abilities, and knowing that we trust each other with more than our lives makes my connection to you unbreakable. Ours is a paranormal connection."

"In this strange world, you're the only person I truly trust."

$\mathcal{L}$incoln Laroque surveyed the piles of personnel folders covering his glass-and-metal desk as if the clear top were thin ice. Many of the workers at Sullivan, Cooper, and Ward Capital would already be polishing up their resumes if they knew what was good for them. Any halfway decent investment analyst would have seen the writing on the wall.

He didn't feel bad for any of the people he was about to fire. Hostile takeovers involved casualties, but unlike war, the victor got to choose who suffered. He pulled the first folder off the chief executives' pile and opened it on his lap. He toyed menacingly with a red Sharpie. His people had left pages of notes in the dossier, regarding the accomplishments, strengths, and weaknesses of the vanquished titan of business. From the cover sheet, a picture of a smug middle-aged businessman smiled at him as if Lincoln were the one being judged.

Lincoln slashed a red X across the entire folder and tossed it on the floor. *Winning should be more fun.*

He would have chalked up his feelings to a midlife crisis had they not plagued him all his adult life. Sitting alone in his penthouse office with its views of the Central Business District out one window and of the French Quarter out the other, he tried to figure out the source of his latest discontent.

Across Canal Street from his modern high-rise stood the marble Greek Revival police station like a chess king's guardian knight. Uncle Gerald ran the department like his own fiefdom, not only within the family but also within the city. No elected politician had the balls to cross him. New Orleans had never been known to have the best handle on crime, and Chief of Police Gerald Laroque used that to his advantage. He manipulated the criminal element like an expert gamesman, pitting them against his foes. Those who screamed the loudest for improved police protection were often those who had run afoul of the secretive chief.

From an early age, Lincoln's mother had made sure he was her brother's favorite nephew. As an adult, however, the ruthless businessman seldom associated with his uncle except at family events. The husky man with the dominating presence might be feared by many who walked New Orleans's streets, but that power had little meaning to Lincoln since city politics no longer interested him.

Like a chess player assessing the strengths and weaknesses of his pieces, Lincoln saw Uncle Gerald as being as useful as a pit bull. Like the man's sons, the LSU linemen, the chief of police had reached the limit of his usefulness once he kept the competition in line.

The light on Lincoln's desk preceded his secretary's voice over the intercom. "It's the bank on line one."

"At least it's a call this time and not a summons. Thanks, Claire."

He pressed the speaker button to keep the matronly voice out of his ear. "What can I do for you, Mother?"

"That last little adventure of yours put quite the dent in your line of credit."

He returned his attention to the French Quarter. Beyond the police station stood the traditional source of the Laroque's power, New Orleans Bank and Trust. Like the brother and sister who ran the two establishments, the bank reflected the same architecturally imposing cold marble exterior as the station. Lincoln's mother, however, wasn't nearly as pliable as her brother.

"Once I have the fat cut out of the investment firm and liquidate their unnecessary assets, the bank will make out just fine," he said. *Like anything I do ever costs the family money.*

"Just don't forget, this establishment isn't your personal piggybank. If you intend to take this big a risk again, I expect to be notified beforehand rather than reading about it in the financial section. I do have other clients to consider." Going up against their ancestor Baron Malveaux had managed to knock her down a few pegs, but she still held the city's purse strings—a fact she liked holding over him as though he were some child demanding too much attention.

"Laroque Enterprises appreciates the notification." Getting under her skin was a skill he'd spent decades perfecting.

"Don't be a little snot. Just because you want to piss away your political career doesn't mean you no longer need me." She hung up before he could respond.

She was the mother bear forever trying to promote her cub, but that mother-son dynamic had ended for him half a lifetime before, and for the first time, he was seeing the woman as vulnerable. The aggressive gene that had been carefully cultivated in their family, and which he had in abundance, argued that the time to pounce had arrived. She could be crushed by any of several means. The tactician, however—and that skill was one he'd had to learn—knew once she was deposed as head of the bank, someone else would take her place. A weakened antagonist might beat an unknown underling with aspirations of power, but in either case, one of his strongest game pieces, the king's proverbial queen, was showing her age.

Leaving her in power wasn't without risk. He'd seen her battle back from too many losses to underestimate her resolve. Since the baron's spirit was locked away, she'd take the opportunity to lick her wounds and come back stronger than ever. He needed to exert his control while he had the chance. His move would need to be decisive, cunning, and noticed by the entire family. Anything less, and he'd be watching his back for her counterstrike.

Unlike in chess, he had to keep a wary eye on his own pieces as well as his adversary's. At any moment, one might decide it was better skilled at handling the reins of power, but for those close to him to be most effective, they had to believe such a possibility was within their grasp.

However, he knew the brother and sister who wielded so much power were themselves under the thumb of the family's ruling elite. That was the shadowy group Lincoln needed to overcome, but not every member was known, even to the rest of the family.

Ignoring the piles of work on his desk, he pulled out a dog-eared notebook from his ever-present briefcase. The front page still had doodles he'd drawn in high school when he was naïve enough to believe his life was his own. Dreams of attending art school and becoming a bohemian painter selling his creations at one of the upscale galleries on Royal Street had been literally knocked out of his head by his mother. *Another life.*

He flipped to his first speculations on who was really pulling the strings. When his distant aunt Mary had become state senator, his attention was drawn to her branch of the family tree. For a few years, they seemed to be on the rise, but as the pendulum of power swung back toward money, he realized the gain had been only temporary. She might remain state senator, but in ten years, she'd moved no farther up the political ladder. In a family of sharks, such lack of progress meant death.

The most logical members of the secret board were his grandparents. He still considered the old coots likely candidates, but their lack of education, grace, and tact argued that some other force was influencing the decisions. Left to those two, the family would more accurately resemble the Beverly Hillbillies.

He flipped the page and saw his first rambling stream-of-consciousness on a paranormal force behind the family's successes. In hindsight, he wasn't as far off as he'd believed back then. Though at the time he thought the idea to be insane, that did lead him to his first meeting with Delphine de Galpion. Although she wasn't much older than he, at the time, those years had equated to a college degree and a shop of her own while he was still worrying about his SATs. Together, they searched through her ancestor's trunks of journals for any mention of his family. They found more than either had bargained for when the mysterious swamp witch made herself known, but in all the intervening years, the creepy old woman had become more legend than fact.

Every page seemed to end in question marks. *If the power really had come from Baron Malveaux, shouldn't that power transfer to me since the cantankerous spirit was locked away in the voodoo fetish? Has it already?* He'd played the game masterfully, secretly drawing forth the spirit, seeing that he possessed that fool of a bartender, pitting him against his mother, then exorcising the demon and locking him away in a form Lincoln could access. Getting the ugly totem out of the hands of his longtime associate was like taking candy from a baby.

He knew he was missing something important. That impression was one that had plagued him most of his life. Never before had his inner compass of caution been more important. He didn't dare attempt to contact Baron Malveaux until all his questions were answered.

Then what? The simple question had proven useful in tempering his ambition. His mother's designs on seeing him achieve political office had been thwarted by his realization that such an achievement would only put him under the thumb of those with money, but following her lead—counting cash and using it as if the world was her Monopoly board—held no interest for him. From an early age, he'd rejected the conclusion that his life could be reduced to a game piece on the board of life.

He stared out the window at the Central Business District. Achieving recognition among the titans of commerce had been his aim in college. Those were the men who changed the lives of common people. Buying businesses, stripping them down to lean, mean, sharklike organizations, and setting those predators loose to do combat to the death used to give him a rush like no other. Workers were the blood cells, management the organs, and he the brains. Politicians provided the playing field, such as it was. In an emergency, the police might act as referees, though, like the politicians, such impartiality was an illusion. Money funded the blood sport. *It should be enough.* However, being the great white shark in a school of makos wasn't enough excitement to last a lifetime. He needed more and always would. *Who knew being at the top of the food chain could be so depressing?*

He turned a hideous statue on a corner of his desk toward himself. "You understood. Taking down an adversary was never enough for you. Eating of their flesh and drinking their blood from their hollowed-out skulls might have been passé, but taking their women for your personal enjoyment—and their humiliation—must have felt like drinking from a victory cup."

His great-great-grandfather's obsession with turning women into whores, however, was also a practice left in the past. Even then, like a drug, the rush only lasted for a moment. *How do I know that?*

Again the questions haunted him. He sat back at his desk and opened the binder to a fresh page to record what he knew.

He wasn't some reincarnation of the baron Malveaux. His ancestor's spirit was locked in the voodoo totem. From the hatred and fear he experienced while looking at the misshapen features of the statue, he knew the baron was his adversary. Though that could easily be explained by the baron's current predicament, the sense of animosity wasn't confined to their recent encounter.

From his research project with Delphine, Lincoln knew of one other member in the history of the family who'd experienced that same hatred. Finding information on the baron's only son wouldn't be easy, but he knew where to start.

He pushed a button on the intercom. "Claire, find me a real-estate firm. I need one that can provide a layer of anonymity between me and the transaction. Make it one we haven't used before."

LINCOLN'S SIX-MONTH-OLD Mercedes S63 Cabriolet fit in nicely on the streets of the Garden District, though he knew no recent resident of the Laurette mansion would have had the money for such an expensive luxury car.

Neighbors were sneaking looks out their windows at the well-tailored businessman like gossipy little old ladies. He did his best to look nonchalant as he approached the weathered front door with its missing panes of glass. If he dawdled, someone might start questioning him about his intentions toward the derelict building. People in historic neighborhoods never did know when to keep their noses out of other people's business.

He didn't have a key, not that one would work in the rusty lock anyway. One good shove of his shoulder as he turned the pitted knob was enough to break through the building's resistance to any intruder.

Lincoln was not unknown to the house. He stood in what had been the grand foyer, surveying the ravages of time. As a child, he'd slid down the two-story wooden banister and received a sound whooping for the joyride. He shook the elegantly carved mahogany railing. The kid he'd been would land on his ass if he tried to slide down it now. *Fucking termites.*

Buying the family mansion from his distant cousin had been simple enough. By hiding behind his shell company and a redevelopment firm, the trail back to him was so convoluted that she hadn't bothered asking any questions about the buyer's identity. Paying cash also had a way of quieting any owner hoping their historic property would retain its past glory while trying to avoid the hassle of fixing up a decaying relic.

Samantha Laurette had been the most direct descendant of Baron Malveaux's only legitimate son and heir, but a little investigating had revealed she had no interest in the family's heritage. The cloak-and-dagger purchase might not have been necessary, but with his family, the less revealed, the better. The need to stay one step ahead had become so ingrained that he hardly noticed the chicanery anymore.

He avoided the downstairs with its once-opulent dining room and outdated kitchen. His great aunt had been a horrendous cook. Even after thirty years, he recalled the smell of her burnt biscuits and gravy. The memory made him nauseated. *How could any woman raised in the South fuck up biscuits?*

The threadbare red carpet runner with its yellow—now brown—flowers, meant to protect the wooden stairs, curled at the edges. Mold tendrils extended beyond the carpet like the black death. He kicked at the rotting wool as if getting back at his relatives for their inhospitality toward the youth he'd once been. Children at the forced family gatherings had been as unwelcome and unnoticed as the peeling paint and wallpaper. Even back then, the place had showed its age.

Lincoln held his breath as he climbed past the second floor. Even decades after her death, his great-grandmother's perfume permeated the walls and carpet. The overly flowery scent made him consider fumigating the house before his next visit.

The rope that had hung from the attic hatch at the end of the third-floor hallway was recently replaced. He figured Samantha had gone through the dusty storage space. Speculating on what family skeletons remained in the dark corners had been a favorite pastime of the family children. Being one of the youngest, he thought his cousins had meant literal bones.

He pulled down the wobbly stairs and ended up covered in dust for his effort. His dry cleaner was going to have a time of it getting the expensive suit back into shape—not that that mattered. If he had to poke around in old trunks and dilapidated rooms, he intended to be comfortable, and that meant a nice suit, not some poor-person jeans.

From the areas clear of dust on the attic floor, he knew anything of value had been removed. He doubted Samantha had found much in the way of compensation for her work. The old folks in his family weren't the type to let expensive heirlooms sit rotting in their closets.

Ambition and money had a way of skipping generations. Anthony Laurette, who had at one time been Antoine-Caliste Malveaux—son of Baron Archibald Malveaux—had that ambition. His architectural firm had designed many of the Garden District's mansions. Unfortunately, his eldest daughter had been too much like her younger sister, Lincoln's grandmother. For each generation that built something of value, another right after it was happy to live off the spoils. Only Laurette's middle son had shown any signs of ambition.

Lincoln pulled a beat-up dining-room chair off a pile and set it under the dormer window. He wasn't there for the plunders of ownership or to get even with his past, at least not the one he remembered. The time had come to find out if the old swamp witch had been right in her prophecy about him so long before or if she was just another con artist out to manipulate him.

He sat in the wobbly chair and put his hands against the solid-wood beams running down from the roof. They wouldn't have changed since the mansion had been built shortly after the War Between the States. He imagined himself being the one drawing up the plans. All his life, people had told him he was an old soul. *If the baron could return from the dead after a century and a half in the ground, could being the reincarnation of his son be that hard to accept?*

After five minutes of intense concentration, he let his arms fall to his sides. He was a titan of business, not a practitioner of voodoo. If his suspicions were true, he was going to need more than this old residence to jump-start the memories. *Damn it!*

He didn't dare try to utilize his ancestor's power, locked in the wooden sculpture, until he knew the truth of his existence. The old man had already proven his lust for control knew no bounds, including family loyalty. Simply being the great-great-grandson wouldn't be enough to keep the baron in check. However, as the only son who had saved generations of the family from the curse brought on by the old goat's lusts, he might have the leverage others had sought.

The attic smelled of past generations, musty, rotting timbers, and death. Connecting to what he believed about himself had only been Plan A. Like any successful businessman, he'd come with a contingency plan.

He stood and kicked the chair over. As the uppermost room of the building—and used only for storage—the attic had suffered the worst from termites and dry rot. The nails holding the beadboard to the rafters weren't doing their job. He pulled on a hanging board, which crumbled in his hand. If need be, he would remove every plank to find what his ancestor had hidden. If the answers to his questions weren't in the diaries left by Marie Laveau—which he had cleverly gotten into the hands of her descendent, Delphine de Galpion—then they must have been in the writings of Anthony Laurette.

Like a squirrel designing a luxury nest, the original founder of Laurette and Associates Architects had an annoying habit of stashing his secrets in the walls of his mansions.

Lincoln pulled hard at a more substantial-looking piece of beadboard, and a splinter pierced his well-manicured index finger. He held his hand up to the light to inspect the wound. Blood quickly ran down his palm and soaked the cuff of his pressed-silk shirt. "Damn it!"

The physical pain paled in comparison to his skiing injuries. Even the loss of the shirt wasn't what bothered him. He had a closet full of them in his office. The old residence and repository of family secrets wasn't going to hand him the answers he sought without a fight, but it had crossed the wrong descendant.

"I'll be back, and I'll have a construction crew at the ready to pull you down, board by board."

3

*K*endell found playing her guitar for Cheesecake had its limitations. Truth be told, the dog didn't have the greatest ear, regarding music. On stage with the band, Kendell was forced to play the rehearsed set list. As Olympia Stain, she could cut loose, but it wasn't *her* music. Myles did his best to be supportive, but like every other boyfriend she'd had, he didn't know how to deliver honest, constructive criticism, and when he did, he was always wrong. The real problem was she needed an audience—one that didn't know her, one with no expectations.

She'd skipped the whole street-performer phase of her education, believing an actual college degree would provide more useful information than being a street urchin playing for coins. As she set up her mobile amplifier on Chartres Street, she wondered if she'd missed something important in her professional calculations. Having tossed countless dollar bills into tip jars, she'd heard every type of busker, from musical virtuosos to dudes who didn't know how to properly handle their instruments. Only once had she attempted that form of baring her musical soul, and she had been under the influence of the voodoo curse at the time.

Though she didn't need the reminder, she placed the three-by-five card with her set list alongside her guitar case. She needed to reduce her music to its most basic elements, and though she bristled at her lack of progress, she knew that meant sticking to other artists' songs. Even worse than that, it meant sticking to strictly instrumental numbers. *Just me and the strings.*

"Classical Gas" had been the first piece she'd mastered on Cecile. She started off slowly, hoping to lose herself in the soft tones of her mellow instrument. Like an old friend serenading her, the piece formed under her fingers as it always had, but playing in public wasn't about staying within her comfort zone. As the number picked up speed, she relied more heavily on the golden pick between her thumb and index finger. She could feel the energy of those around her funneling through her fingers to the pick, which moved at lighting speed over the strings. As with playing under the curse, the power was addictive. She transitioned to Paul Simon's "Anji" without realizing it. By Link Wray's "Rumble," she had a young kid banging on a five-gallon bucket as accompaniment. She didn't need the help, but his youthful, uninhibited energy fit in well with her strumming.

When she finally set the guitar down, the pick was blazing hot between her fingers, and Cecile's strings looked like frayed twine. The applause was loud and heartfelt, but adulation wasn't her goal. She had felt the crowd's energy flowing through her like electricity through a wire. The performance had melded them to her, and as it did, she came to know each person on a level that transcended the lives they knew.

An old man with a beat-up trumpet approached her as the crowd thinned out. "Pretty good playing for a little white girl. You are the one who performed in front of Jackson Square, aren't you? I kept expecting to see you play again. Did the *man* offer you fame and fortune?"

Lincoln Laroque's help in securing Polly Urethane and the Stripper's gig at Jazz Fest had indeed come on the heels of her solo exhibitionism.

"Something like that," she said.

"Since you're back here, maybe that wasn't the success you were seeking."

The event had shown her how a large crowd could act like jet fuel for her playing, but the barrage of emotions made it hard to define who she wanted to be behind the guitar. "Every gig is different. So long as I'm growing as an artist, I enjoy the diversity."

He pulled out a bent-up card and handed it to her. "Come by on Friday at midnight, and give the doorman this card—if you've got the nerve."

She read the heading on the tattered business card: Cutting Heads.

~

THE WAREHOUSE on Rampart Street wasn't in the best part

of town. Kendell seldom had reason to wander beyond the Bywater, and never at night. Had it not been for the ever-present homeless population, who always had her back, she wouldn't have found the nerve, but she knew her constant companions would always keep an eye out for her safety. She swung her yellow Vespa around the corner of the nondescript warehouse and parked it with other bikes and scooters.

What am I doing here? Music had held a unique magical attraction to her for as long as she could remember, but never before had that passion led her to reckless endangerment.

An old man sat on a stool leaning back against the corrugated metal wall. "Have you got the chops to enter?"

"I suppose we'll find out." She pulled out the creased business card and handed it over.

He hitched his thumb toward the door. "Don't take it too hard if you don't last long. Few first-timers do."

She wasn't sure if he was trying to intimidate her or ease her upcoming self-doubt. "What are the rules?"

"Anyone is free to challenge anyone else. If you don't accept, you'll be asked to leave. Lose a competition, and you can hang around to learn something or try again."

She clutched the handle of the guitar case. "What about the stakes?"

"The one challenged gets to set them. People play for anything from a buck to an instrument, but it has to be something you have on you. We don't want to hunt people down for nonpayment."

She wished she'd brought more things a musician might

want, but that would have made her more of a target in the iffy neighborhood. "Who decides the winner?"

"The crowd has a say, but to relieve undue popular bias, the old bluesmen make the final decisions."

"And so long as I don't refuse a challenge, I can stay as long as I want?"

He leaned forward, causing the wooden stool to land with a crack on the cement sidewalk. "Them's the rules. As you're a first timer, stick close to the door, and you can watch for a while to figure out who's who in there. The closer you get to the center of the warehouse, the more intense the competition."

He opened the metal door for her. The wall of sound inside made concentrating hard. With so many instruments playing so many pieces, the scene more accurately resembled a battle than a concert. She looked away from the activity to mentally catch her breath. A line of floats from the Krewe of Boo filled one wall. Though much simpler in design than the tractor-drawn trailers used for Mardi Gras, the dayglow-painted sides and paper-mache goblins gave the small floats a feeling of whimsy missing from the more commercial floats. Paintings were stacked against the sides of the oversized wagons, rope harnesses hung from the rafters, and the whole place smelled of cannabis, incense, and sex. The space evidently had many uses. She couldn't count the musicians facing off against each other. Between the noise and the crowd, she wondered how anyone could identify the activities as competitions.

The man who'd given her the card on Chartres was sitting on the hood of a rusted, broken-down taxi, looking out at the action. "Give it some time. You'll figure out where you want to be. The drummers stick to the back area. Otherwise, it's just a mixture of instruments. Those who've been doing this for a time will form up groups for more intense competitions. Don't fall for it, though, if they invite you to join. They call it strip shredding. I've had to round up more than one overcoat for some poor naked girl who didn't have the chops."

"Thanks for the warning."

He pointed toward a teenage boy who was adjusting his strings. "When you're ready, you can start off challenging Slick. He likes playing for dollar bills. The kid's got skills, but he hates feeling pressured. By waiting for others to make the first move, he gets to keep the wager limited. Just watch out when he starts pulling his double-or-nothing routine on you. It violates the rules of the challenge as he's both requesting and dictating the stakes, but you have the right to say no in that situation."

She took her time, watching the musical styles of those playing around her. Loud head-slamming guitarists who played with testosterone and little else tended to compete with each other. The way they jumped and cavorted reminded her of playing under the influence of the curse. She could have blown them all away if she had just one of the baron's cufflinks, but that wasn't how she wanted to be remembered. More classically trained musicians found benches in the ghoulish art floats so their refined licks could be appreciated. Though they had skill, she didn't hear much passion.

Interspersed between the players, each decked out as a

stage persona, were old men in rumpled street clothes. Though they didn't seem so destitute as to appear homeless, their weathered faces and worn suits contrasted starkly to those trying to outdo each other in every way possible. She watched one old man step between two headbangers. Instead of being thrust out of the way for his impertinence, the two guitarists respectfully set aside their instruments to listen to his judgement. Polite applause went up from the audience when he indicated the winner.

Slick hadn't paired off yet in competition. Like her, he seemed to be taking the temperature of the room and distinguishing the real competitors from those just out to strut their stuff.

She tried to stay out of his eyeline while she moved closer. "Care to show a girl what you've got?"

Without turning to her, he pulled out a crumpled dollar bill from his jeans and tossed it on the floor. "You start."

Not having heard him play, she wasn't sure what to lay down. Then again, she was the one doing the challenging. She plugged in her black electric guitar to the nearest available amp and plucked out a riff from "Come as You Are."

She only made it a few bars in before he picked up the musical phrase and added in some rhythm guitar.

By not singing along, she had the freedom to let her guitar emulate the words. With a generic pick between her fingers, she began playing with style.

Instead of competing, Slick seemed intent on discovering the limits of her skills. By taking both rhythm and lead, he left her to explore other aspects of the song.

Kurt Cobain's soulful voice wasn't one that she could copy, but her fingers discovered on her strings the feeling he poured into the lyrics.

Just when things were getting interesting, a man pointed his cane at Slick. The competition had ended, and she'd lost, not that she disagreed with the ruling. The kid had a subtle style that stayed with Kendell even after the sound of the guitars faded away.

"Congratulations," she said.

He picked up the two bucks. "Push yourself harder, not louder. Steer clear of the metalheads. And whatever you do, stay out of Reggie's way. He's got a wall full of guitars he's won off the uninitiated."

"Thanks for the advice."

She held her own in the next competition but still lost another dollar in the end. Most of the musicians in the room seemed more intent on discovering their opponent's vulnerabilities than taking what meager possessions they had on them. At least, that was her impression for the first hour.

The loud metalheads were the first to sit in the stands or find the door. That type of playing, especially in competition, had a way of fraying strings and muscles. Next to go were the classically trained. She sympathized with their haggard expressions of frustration. They probably were better skilled than most in the room, but the bluesmen weren't looking for technical proficiency. Playing with soul took more than hitting the strings just right. In fact, that usually resulted in pretty stale renditions.

Kendell was in the thick of it when she heard haunting

strumming from the center of the room. Listening to someone she thought must be an old-time bluesman, she dropped the riff she'd been playing.

She felt as if she was being pulled in by a magnet as she squeezed between the onlookers to see a busker working his magic on a beat-up thrift-store guitar. The instrument had to be older than the boy playing it. She thought at any minute he would strike a string so hard the bridge would come flying off the bottom.

She calmed her thoughts in an attempt to read any dark energy that might explain the music, but the competition ended too soon. Without realizing what she was doing, she slung her guitar into place. "I'd like to see you do that again."

Before he accepted her challenge, his previous victim handed him his guitar as payment.

"I only play for instruments."

Looking at the cheaply made guitar with more lacquer missing than covering the wood, she wondered why anyone would challenge him for such a piece of crap, but from the half dozen guitars behind him, she knew better than to underestimate her opponent. *At least I didn't bring Cecile.* "Doesn't seem like a fair trade."

"Little girl, this here's a Kalamazoo KG-14. Story goes, this here box was owned by Robert Johnson hisself. Now, as the man died poor and unappreciated, no one knows for sure, but from the way she cuts heads, the legend has taken hold. Either that or I'm just a damn fine guitar player."

Slick leaned in next to her. "I warned you."

She'd left the gold guitar pick at home. Flashing such an expensive and powerful object would have only made her a mark for the competitors—or someone less respectable when she left the warehouse. Her goal was to learn what she could do, but for the kid to have won so many high-priced guitars, the wreck he was playing must have had some magic in the strings. The deck was stacked, and all she could do was play the hand she'd been dealt.

She figured any established piece of music would only look like an opening chess gambit that had too many ways of being countered. She attempted to replicate the notes Cheesecake made when Kendell had been gone for too long.

Reggie added in a polyphonic counterpoint as easily as she might switch from strumming to picking.

Classically trained. She built a melodic counterpoint that switched the random notes into something that began to resemble a song.

A half hour passed, with each of them modifying, cutting, and expanding the piece and neither admitting defeat or claiming victory. Three bluesmen stood nearby, but they also reserved judgement.

At last, Reggie strummed three hard notes to announce the end, took off his guitar, and handed it to her. "Congratulations. You beat me fair."

You'll probably claim to be playing B. B. King's Lucille next time. "It was an education."

～

BACK IN HER APARTMENT, Kendell tried a few numbers on the old guitar. It played well enough for a beater. It couldn't match Cecile for sound quality, and it would never hold up to intense use, but it had a uniquely tortured tone. As she caressed its battered top, she wondered if a guitar from a famous musician would be obvious to anyone or would appear no different from a dime-store find.

Myles leaned against the doorframe of her bedroom. "That has to be the ugliest instrument I've ever seen." For all his ability to read past energy, he had no clue about what made a musical instrument beautiful.

"I won it last night at Cutting Heads."

He walked over and sat on the bed next to her. "I've heard a few of the bar band members mention that place. From what I've gathered, it can be kind of rough."

Once the competition had started, she hadn't given much thought to her safety. "The regulars there are serious about music. Anyone unfamiliar with the place, thinking they could walk in and make a quick reputation for themselves, would be delusional."

"Forgive me for asking, but is that guitar something I should congratulate you on? Seems like I should be asking what the runner-up took home—worn-out strings, maybe?"

"Very funny." She handed him the beat-up instrument. "Tell me what you see."

He turned it from side to side while peering into the sound hole. "Well, I can tell you it's been played by a lot of people. I guess it doesn't take much psychometric skill to see that, though."

Their relationship had been better since their late-night talk on the veranda, but when it came to delving into the past, he was still like someone home from the hospital and not willing to get back on his feet.

"I'd never push you," she said, "but I thought we could take one of your spiritual journeys with this thing. I don't detect any dark energy like with the Malveaux-curse objects. And I understand musicians, so I can figure out what we might witness. I can help, but only if you want me to."

His knuckles turned white as he gripped the guitar neck like a snake he was trying to keep from biting him. "What are you hoping to discover?"

"In all likelihood, we'll just see a series of street performers, but the guy I won this from said it belonged to Robert Johnson. Honestly, I don't believe that's true, but I am curious."

He eased up his grip and started inspecting the scratches and dents. "And if it is true, and he really did sell his soul to the devil? Once a person dies and crosses from Guinee to the *deep waters*, any human energy left in an object is locked in place. For me, reading that energy is like witnessing a recording of events. The experience is still very emotional, but the person involved isn't present. That's not the case if that person is still in Guinee."

"That's two pretty big ifs. First, this probably is just an old beat-up guitar with no historical significance. Second, even if it did belong to Mr. Johnson, and he really did sell his soul to the devil, who's to say he ended up in Guinee? Besides, Guinee was never the problem. The loas of the dead that guard the afterlife have been good to both of us. And now that Baron Malveaux is trapped in the voodoo totem, he's no longer a threat to you."

The way Myles ran his hands over the beat-up wood led

her to guess he was still searching out any vestige of hostile energy. "Isolating one individual would be tough."

"He didn't play like other musicians. What recordings remain of his are filled with pure, distilled emotion."

Myles set the guitar against the bed. "Assuming the most unlikely case and we do meet him, what's your plan?"

Rescuing the bluesman from a fate worse than death hadn't entered her thoughts. "He wouldn't be in the same category as the baron's women. They were held against their will. He sold his soul for the recognition he currently enjoys."

"There's a lot of words in that sentence that sound like loopholes to me. He died poor and unappreciated. If he's in Guinee, his current reputation might not matter much to him. Though I don't consider the place hell, having been trapped there, I can see how others might. I don't want to end up pissing off another devil."

Kendell's focus was refined by Myles's arguments. "I won't lie—saving souls excites me. I can't do it alone, though." She pulled out the golden guitar pick. "It's not exactly an invitation, but the loas have expressed their gratitude. That has to count for something, should we get into mischief."

~

KENDELL LAY on her bed next to Myles with the guitar on top of them. She held his hand. Cheesecake snuggled up against their feet. In the past, Kendell's biggest concern had been letting Myles down by not being able to let go of her life the way he'd explained, but her attention wasn't turned inward at present. Even before their souls bonded in the realm beyond life, she could feel his anxiety as if it were her own.

She focused fully on him, letting her awareness merge with his. Myles, the rational, strong adult, stood guard over the scared and misunderstood boy he'd never quite outgrown. The journey into the vast reservoir of human consciousness, which he used to wade into like stepping into a cold lake on a hot day, more closely resembled a child's first experience at the top of a log-flume ride. She could feel his apprehension building, but his steely inner command quieted his thoughts and focused them both on the guitar.

In her other hand, she held the golden guitar pick. The trip into the instrument's past would be up to Myles, but if they ran into any unexpected demon, she wanted to be prepared. He'd risked enough for her curiosity, and though she'd saved him from the baron, she wasn't blameless—even if he didn't hold her responsible.

Suddenly, faces, street corners, and countless dollar bills spun past her as though she was in the center of a demented musical-performance tornado. When the chaos settled, she stood on a dry, dusty road cutting through a parched field of dying grass. Though Myles was a part of her awareness, he remained in the background like a child watching from his room at the end of a hallway.

A man younger than she'd expected sat on a flat rock in the parched landscape. His torn and dirty clothes matched the countryside in color and deprivation.

A lump formed in her throat. *How am I supposed to talk to a legend?* "Are you Robert Johnson?"

The man looked up with a start. Though his body had the thin athleticism of youth, his dark, sorrowful eyes reminded her of the pictures she'd seen of the sage bluesman. "Where'd you come from?"

She looked around the empty plain. Even if she could have walked that far, dust would have been kicked up from her shoes into the still air, betraying her approach.

"I suppose I'm a ghost," she said.

He nodded as if what she'd said sounded perfectly plausible. "If you've come to take my life, you're welcome to it."

"What if I were to tell you your future isn't as bleak as your past?"

He turned his guitar back and forth against the dirt.

So that's where those scratches on the bottom came from.

"All I care about is playing, and not even my friends will let me on stage anymore. What good is a musician if he drives people away? A man's work is only relevant if others appreciate it."

She'd experienced that same self-pity a time or two, but seeing it in another, she vowed to never again succumb to its influence. "Find another emotion—one the audience will respond to. Stop acting like you're the only one in the room. No one cares about another's melancholy. They care about their own."

He stopped playing with his guitar and gave her a good, long stare. "What would you know about it?"

"I've played a gig or two. You're out of sync with your

listeners. You act like they owe you their attention. Who are you to preach to them?"

He turned back to his guitar. "I just want to be remembered as playing with heart."

"You have it in you, but stop thinking it's in you alone. Find your emotional connection to other people. You're a bluesman. Give your soul to every performance."

"And in exchange for my soul, you'll give me musical immortality?"

The dry landscape seemed to have infected her throat. All she'd meant to do was have a conversation and maybe help him out of a bind. The last thing she wanted was to end up playing the role of the legend's devil.

"I'm just a fellow musician trying to give you some hope," she said.

He pointed at Cheesecake, the protector wolf at her side. "The original trickster with her hellhound. I'm not so easily fooled by the cover of a pretty woman. Though I suppose I've got nothing left to lose. Teach me how to play such that people will listen."

How am I supposed to respond? "I'm not the devil. I'm from the future"? How would that affect his playing? Cheesecake the hellhound sat at attention. So many songs had been written about that very encounter. *Who am I to change musical history?*

"Let your being meld with humanity," she said. "Don't just play using your emotions. Tap into that reservoir of hurt and longing, and realize we all drink from the same source. Don't focus on your playing but on your existence."

For an hour, they discussed the finer points of

connecting to an audience and the power that resonated from the live encounter versus the sterile environment of a recording studio. Being on the other side of life, she could share what little she actually knew of tapping into humanity's subconscious even when separated from people.

She could feel the connection to the unknown weakening. Like a vampire who didn't know when to stop sucking the lifeblood from a victim, she'd held Myles in his psychometric trance for too long. The young black guitarist began picking "Crossroads" on his weathered instrument. It wasn't quite the song she remembered, but he was well on his way.

Even Cheesecake looked drained as the three of them came back to full consciousness on her bed. Though the old girl enjoyed her naps in the sun, Kendell could tell the difference between normally lazy and spiritually exhausted.

Myles struggled to sit up. "Did you find what you were looking for?"

She shivered in a cold sweat. "Was that Guinee or the *deep waters*? Have I become a version of the devil?"

Myles petted Cheesecake's shaggy coat as she looked up at Kendell with her kind, loving eyes. "Time only makes sense to the living. Recorded events left in physical objects like this guitar happen when an intense emotional experience infects the molecules. Because Robert Johnson was a young man, I'd tend to believe it was more a recording than an actual conversation."

"It felt so real."

He set the guitar on the floor. "When I'm experiencing an object's history, I often end up feeling what the main character was going through. I don't often play the role of the antagonist, but I suspect that's what happened to you."

"But the words were my own. I believed everything I said about connecting to an audience and giving my soul to a performance. If that was also the devil's argument to Robert, doesn't that make us the same?"

"When it comes to what's truly good and what's evil, I'm not sure what to believe anymore."

The guitar pick in her hand radiated warmth throughout her body.

*a*s Lincoln walked down Bourbon Street, he did his best to avoid the plastic cups and alcohol-soaked strings of beads littering the sidewalk. The potholed street wasn't much better, but he only had to walk around the cars, whose drivers had ill-advisedly gotten stuck in the traffic jam that never eased. Though the occupants of the stationary vehicles might not be any soberer than the weaving pedestrians, at least they weren't able to swerve into him.

He wasn't a fan of visiting the French Quarter. Not only were his uncle and mother's mausoleum-like establishments there, but the streets were filled with tourists and lined with garish buildings that looked ready to fall down. Business meetings were better conducted in comfort, where a lackey could fetch the participants whatever they desired, not in some smoke-filled bar or, worse, an opponent's home turf.

He hoped the show of contrition would soften Delphine up to his request.

I friggin' should have had my driver bring me. He knew, though, that would have turned the fifteen-minute walk into an hour of people gawking in the darkened windows of his town car.

He turned off Bourbon Street toward the quieter residential section of the Quarter. Only the peeling paint on the building looked to have changed in the thirty years since his last visit to Scratch and Sniff perfumery. Five in the afternoon was still a little early for a shop that specialized in fragrances mild enough to be used under a stripper's G-string, but Lincoln's time was too valuable to wait. He hammered on the weather-beaten wall.

Delphine opened the door. Her tired look of exasperation lasted only for a moment. "What are you doing here?"

"I *was not* just in the neighborhood. I came to see if you've made any progress on the Marie Laveau journals I gave you."

She pulled her Haitian wrap tight around herself and stood aside so he could enter. "I didn't realize a translation was part of the agreement. I gave you your ancestor trapped in the totem, and in exchange I got my ancestor's writings."

Lincoln's eyes watered and nose burned at the smells of too many conflicting perfumes. "Our history goes further back than one business transaction. You know what I want."

She motioned for him to sit at her worktable while she took the grand African-motif throne. "I can't tell you how to control the baron's spirit. I wouldn't even if I could. The diaries are filled with the incantations Marie used, along with the terms of the arrangements. If she'd anticipated the baron being enticed out of Guinee and trapped in a totem, she didn't write about it."

He'd figured as much, just as he knew claiming ignorance would be Delphine's opening gambit. "I've read what little I could of the diaries. She mentioned a *curse guardian*, and I think we've both met her."

Delphine pulled one of the journals from the bookshelf behind her. "You think she meant the swamp witch?"

"It would explain why that old woman took such an interest in me. I'm betting you know where to find her."

She ran her long, elegant fingers over the leather binding. "Marie was careful to keep her guardians well hidden. Some aren't even among the living. Kendell and Myles believed the women's souls the baron held captive in Guinee were the Malveaux curse guardians. With the baron captured, the women have been freed to move on to the *deep waters*, thus ending the curse."

"A nice story. One I'm sure you fostered."

"Those two were beginning to see this place as a twenty-four, seven information desk. Giving them a mission meant I could get back to my business."

Lincoln understood very well about giving someone what they thought they wanted as a means of getting them off his back. He had enjoyed playing with Kendell's musical aspirations like a child dangling a ball of string in front of a kitten. *Sexy little minx.* "It also meant they did most of the work in drawing forth the baron." He held up his wrists to show Delphine the baron's old cufflinks. "You and I both know the curse isn't ended. These chunks of metal still mean me harm."

She flashed him the same cross look he remembered as a boy searching through her trunks for information about his family. "Those aren't toys."

"Teasing an opponent into thinking they have the upper hand often has a way of exposing their weaknesses. My point is someone is still standing watch over the curse."

"Assuming you're right about that old woman, what would you hope to learn from her?"

The memory of the swamp witch's blind blue-white eyes still unnerved him. "You told me back then that she was an oracle, and she called me the family's fulfillment. It didn't mean much to me then, but now that I have the baron, I need answers. If you can't tell me what I need to know, maybe she can."

"Even if it were that old hag, she must be long dead by now."

Thirty years before, Delphine's tactics of distraction might have worked on him, but he'd participated in too many hostile board meetings to be so easily dissuaded.

"Then someone will have taken her place," he said. "I have the resources to drain every bayou in a hundred-mile radius to flush her out."

She was clearly weighing her options, which meant he'd already won. "It would be best if you didn't. She's a Wiccan High Priestess. Marie liked to use opposing forces to keep her spells in check. Wicca and voodoo mix about as well as oil and water. The last thing New Orleans needs is an interparanormal war."

"Then come with me. Make the introduction. We'll both hear what she has to say." Dangling the prospect of retaining some control over a situation had tripped up more than one of his opponents.

~

LINCOLN KNEW he could have an airboat out on the jetty off Interstate 55 in half an hour. From there, they could skim across the water hyacinths and be out to the cypress swamp in another hour. The whole excursion could be completed in half a day, and he'd still have time for meetings in his office. However, that wasn't how things were done in rural Louisiana. Flashing a lot of cash was likely to alienate the locals, and the swamp witch wasn't exactly findable on GPS. As it was, his brand-new Levi's and fresh-from-the-package T-shirt made him stand out like a city-slicker con man. Even the year-old Ford Expedition made him feel like a wannabe adventurer. At least it wasn't as showy as the Mercedes.

Delphine did the talking to the fishermen and crawfish trappers. "I'm looking for someone who can navigate the tributaries without a motor. I need to get deep into the Honeydew bayou—out to the cypress grove. If you know the area, you probably know who I'm looking to find."

None of the mud-stained men gave her much attention as they loaded their small outboard motorboats with gear. Even Lincoln knew the area wasn't to be attempted by anyone unfamiliar with the myriad of creeks, islands, and marshes. He'd probably get lost after the first bend in the river.

Delphine leaned against the grill of his SUV. "Now, we wait."

"For what?"

She nodded toward the men pushing off their small aluminum boats for a hot, muggy, mosquito-filled day on the water. "Those guys might not seem very chatty, but they're worse than an old wives' club when it comes to gossiping out on the water. There's not a lot to do while waiting for mudbugs to find their way into the traps. The people we're looking for can't be approached by car. Word will have to seep into the swamp like fresh water let in from the spillway. If no one contacts us by two this afternoon, we'll head back to town and try again tomorrow."

He looked at her in disbelief. "I expected to have this wrapped up by this evening."

"You expected wrong. Even if we do find the swamp witch, she'll want us to stay the night as our rite of passage. Assume for a minute that you're right about her being the custodian of the Malveaux curse. Do you really think she's just going to give up her secrets because you ask? Better start thinking about how to convince her because money or threats aren't going to work. She'll have the specter of Marie Laveau hanging over her head."

All he'd been focusing on was finding the old woman. Convincing her to talk hadn't entered his equation. "She said I was the fulfillment. That has to count for something."

"Don't bet on it. From what I remember, she wasn't swayed by conversation involving logic."

They had time with little else to do but talk, so he seized the opportunity. "How well do you know her?"

Delphine's heavy sigh indicated the topic wasn't unexpected. "I first met her not long after my mother moved us back to New Orleans from Haiti. I must have been about six years old. Even then, I thought that witch was old. She was probably younger than I am now."

"Did you come out to the swamp?"

Delphine stared out at the water. "No. She found us. Mother wanted to keep a low profile when it came to Marie's descendants until she knew the various factions of the family. By being nonthreatening, she was able to buy up a lot of Marie's journals without eliciting much suspicion—not that my tourist-obsessed charlatan relatives gave a rat's ass about our family's history. One day, I came home from school and found the swamp witch sitting in our parlor like she owned the place. The way mother doted on her, I figured she had to be important. Of course, they didn't discuss anything in front of me. I was just a child."

"Did she become a regular visitor?"

Delphine's laugh had a sarcastic edge to it. "Hardly. I didn't see her again until I was in high school. She's been like a phantom in my life. I think she just likes checking in to see if I'm still here."

"You mean in New Orleans?"

"I mean in life. Each time I look in her eyes, it's like she expects me to be dead. I can't explain it. It's like she's trying to burn me to the ground just by turning those dead orbs at me."

He hadn't considered how much Delphine might dread

the excursion. Then again, he seldom worried much about what others thought or felt when he was on a quest. "Then there was the time I met her with you."

"You put too much stock in that meeting. She's not a voodoo priestess. Me saying she's an oracle is like you saying someone's good with numbers. You use that person to get an insight into another business that you're not familiar with to gain an edge, but you don't envy their position. Wicca is more like a predecessor of science. They think they can see energy currents moving through plants and animals."

"If you don't believe in it, why did you make me promise never to discuss the meeting?"

Delphine shrugged. "You were a kid who wanted to be an artist. I'd hoped by not talking about her, you might forget her. Wouldn't you have been happier not following what your family wanted of you?"

"So you think her comment worked to change my life's direction?"

She turned to survey the horizon though no boats were answering their call. "Hasn't it? You've grown more obsessed with your family's source of power every year. Now that you think you've captured it, you're looking for the user's manual on what to do with it. Since I can't instruct you, you're hoping this hermit of a witch might."

He had to confess she wasn't wrong. "What does it mean to be a guardian? What will she know about the curse?"

"You're talking advanced voodoo. Marie knew some of her spells would last generations. By handing one set of facts to one faction, like the diaries she left her descendants, and putting other information in the hands of the opposition, she ensured someone would always be around in case something went wrong. By design, I have no idea what she knows—if anything."

~

FOR THREE DAYS, they returned to the same jetty, asked the same questions, and got the same lack of response. He began to believe Delphine was right. The old woman had probably died so long before that no one knew what they were talking about, and if any of the men did know anything, they wouldn't admit to the swamp horror stories away from a good campfire.

As the sun again passed over the top of his Ford, he considered giving up on the idea of finding the swamp witch.

"You folks serious about going out to Honeydew?"

He turned and saw a man standing on a wooden flatboat, a pole in his hand.

"Can you get us there?" Lincoln asked.

"Not many venture into that wilderness. Those that do seldom find their way out. I only traverse those waterways during the day. No one in their right mind would stay past sunset."

Delphine left the cool confines of the air-conditioned SUV. "We're looking for the swamp witch. Can you take us to her?"

"Nope. Though I can drop you off on the far side of her

island. You'll have to find your way from there. My territory doesn't extend to her side of the bayou."

Delphine lifted her pack from the back seat. "We'll be spending the night there. If your offer includes picking us up tomorrow, we can leave immediately."

"Don't remember making an offer, but if you're serious, it's going to cost you."

Lincoln pulled the billfold from the pocket of his jeans. "Name your price."

Having settled on a dollar figure that would allow the boatman to upgrade his raft to a nicely appointed aluminum skiff, Lincoln helped Delphine to a seat at the front of the old-fashioned boat. "I didn't realize anyone used poles to get around the bayous anymore."

The man stood at the back and used the long rod for both propulsion and steering. "No one does except me. The deep cypress groves are murder on outboard engines, and airboats end up skewered on cypress knees like pigs on a spit. The closer you get to that witch's island, the pointier the knees. She doesn't like visitors. She's also not a fan of noise, so once we get close, I'd keep quiet if I were you."

As Lincoln had suspected, he lost his bearings before the boat even left the winding river. Once in the heart of the swamp, he started praying their ride would honor his agreement to pick them up the next day. Should he decide not to, they didn't have much hope of ever being found.

Dusk had fallen by the time the man beached the flat-bottom boat.

"Head through those trees," he said. "The island's not big, but it can be disorienting. If you get lost, just head in a straight line until you hit the swamp again. If you find yourself in the cypress grove, you're in the witch's property. Otherwise, you'll be where I can find you. I'll be back in the morning. Be ready for me. I'm not waiting around."

The moment Lincoln pulled their packs from the boat, the man shoved off and was headed away from the island.

"Any thoughts on reaching the witch without making ourselves unwelcome?"

Delphine slung her backpack over her shoulders. "This place is covered in spells. I can smell them. She knows we're here. If we head straight across the island, we'll either find her or end up ensnared in one of her confounding curses and wander around lost until she decides we've had enough."

He had to hurry to keep up with her. His temptation to fill the time with conversation was tempered by the boatman's warning about keeping quiet. The silence, however, only added to his feelings of dread at the island becoming his final resting place.

The wax myrtles mixed in with the red maples made for slow going. If a path existed somewhere on the island, they'd missed it. He could hear animals lurking in the shadows but had trouble identifying the shrieks and howls.

"What are you two doing on my land?"

He turned and saw a woman in her early twenties pointing a shotgun at their feet. His shock gave Delphine the opening to answer.

"We're searching for the swamp witch that lives here. She knows who I am."

The young woman's matted blond hair cascaded down

her shoulders as she nodded. "Follow me, and keep up. I don't want to have to come back out to find you again."

She moved through the forest like a deer following a barely detectable trail. Shrubs that she skirted around managed to reach out and snag Lincoln's pants, though, from the holes in her tight, faded jeans, he guessed her proficiency had come at a price.

The island's scrub forest gave way to towering cypress trees that grew out of the bog. His fear of being scratched by the bushes was replaced by that of sinking into the marshy ground. In the distance, a house nestled in the limbs of the trees. It looked as though a hurricane had deposited it high off the ground.

"My grandmother is waiting. I'll be back in the morning." The mysterious woman disappeared back into the forest before he had a chance to respond.

Delphine put her hands on her hips and arched her back as she looked up at the boards that had been nailed to a tree trunk to form a ladder. "I'm getting too old for this nonsense."

"Maybe this is why she doesn't stop by your shop more often. I can't imagine making this trek if I didn't have to. I'll bet she hasn't been down from that perch in decades."

She gave him a side glance. "You don't have to go up there. This whole excursion is just to satisfy your damn curiosity."

She didn't understand. Once a question was fully formed in Lincoln's mind, he'd stop at nothing to find the answer.

"I'll go first to make sure the trunk isn't rotted out or something," he said.

"Cypress doesn't rot, but I'm not going to stop your show of chivalry."

His muscles were already aching from the jog through the forest. He put his foot on the lowest board and slowly trusted his weight to it. *One down, twelve to go. In any civilized forest, this tree ladder would have had a maximum-age-and-weight-limit warning.* Only children would find the island obstacle course anything other than torture, though, even as a kid, Lincoln would have avoided the adventure at all costs.

At the top of the ladder, he pushed open the hatch over his head, which fell with a loud thud onto the porch. The wood planks, along with the rest of the house, tilted unnervingly toward the ground. A drunk wouldn't have a chance, but being sober, he found the front door without losing his footing.

"You've come all this way. You might as well come in," someone with a raspy voice said inside the house.

Lincoln pulled on the screen door, which appeared to have been slashed by some rabid animal. From the way the tears stretched from the upper corner to below his knees, that had to have been one impressive creature.

His first impression of the living room was that it had been abandoned for decades. Dust coated every surface. The only colors he could make out were shades of blue and gray. He peered into the various mismatched high-back chairs for the lone occupant.

What he'd at first dismissed as a pile of rags shifted in the dim light let in from a side window. "Have a seat."

Once he'd located a chair he thought might not crumble under him or leave him covered in magically cursed dust, he noticed Delphine standing in the doorway. He stared at her, expecting her to enter, but she stood stiff, as if bolted to the floor.

The old woman's voice sounded as dry and harsh as the dust that burned his throat. "Don't worry about your friend. There exists a separation between voodoo priestess and witch. Though the distinction may seem a matter of semantics to the uninitiated, Miss de Galpion knows her place." The swamp witch leaned forward out of the shadows. Her gray skin stretched thin over her bones, leaving him the impression of a living mummy. Wisps of white hair inadequately covered her freckled scalp.

Though Lincoln found the scene disquieting at first, he'd survived much more terrifying encounters in hostile boardrooms. "Do you remember me?"

"Lincoln, son of Margery and Harrison Laroque." She waved a bony finger at him. "Your lineage is written all over your face. I met you once as a young man. The years have left their mark on you."

He'd never begrudged the gray hair at his temples or the lines on his forehead. Like most men in the business world, he relished the signs of command. "You said something to me back then."

"I set you on a course that led you here today. My question now is, are you ready, or do you still need time to mature?"

"I run one of the biggest—"

"I don't give a mosquito's testicle for what you do," she interrupted. "Your successes in life only fog the truth."

What he needed no longer lay on the line his life had followed. "What is the truth?"

"I can read your aura, oracle the future, and hold the past's secrets, but a person's truth lies within them. Never let anyone claim to know more about your true being than you know about yourself."

Just perfect. All this way for a bullshit answer. "You called me the family's fulfillment. What did you mean?"

"You didn't really come all this way to ask about a comment I made thirty years ago. What do you want?"

The time for small talk was over. "I have the imprisoned spirit of Baron Archibald Malveaux. Tell me how to use it."

"You think this is some little trinket you keep on your desk for your personal amusement? Like you can just push a button and make it dance to your tune? You are a fool."

Even as a child, he'd quickly lost interest in toys. "I think it's a power capable of creating real change in people's lives."

She waved her leathery hand at him and scoffed. "Pretty words with no meaning. Your mother was right. You would have made a good politician. Try again."

"I think it has the power to make a change in *my* life."

"That goes without saying. If all you seek is change, I'll see that you slip going down the stairs out there. A fall from up here could have quite the *impact* on your life." She filled the room with screeching laughter at her own joke.

He didn't find her amusing. "I have power over a lot of people. With or without the old baron's abilities, I plan on increasing my reach. One day, that might stretch all the way out to this bayou."

"You would already resort to threats? I thought you had

more imagination. What you have in that totem is more than power. It's more like a magnet that attracts power. It's the realization of ambition distilled out from countless conquests. Like any other force in nature, power gravitates to the winner."

He could feel her influence taking hold of him, preventing him from playing his usual game of deception. "That's what I crave. It's my birthright. You said I was the family's fulfillment. This is what you meant. I know it is."

"What you seek is only the beginning. The game Malveaux began never reached an end. His craving lives on."

He saw his opening. "If I'm not the one to claim his energy, someone else will. Though Malveaux can't escape the totem, that much command can't stay locked up forever. The day will come when someone tries to utilize what they've found. Isn't it better to open Pandora's box in a controlled environment?"

"You play an interesting game, Lincoln Laroque. I'm an old woman. You tempt me with one last bite at the apple of guardianship, but you don't fool me. You believe you can defeat me once you've gotten what you want."

He knew the dynamics she was weighing. As an old woman with knowledge and power, she might prove a better adversary than her youthful, uninitiated granddaughter. The old swamp witch would fear that once she had passed, Lincoln might have a much easier time convincing the younger witch to do his bidding.

She settled back into the chair so deeply he wondered if she would be lost to sight in the ghostly shadows. "It's getting late. There's a cot in the next room and a hammock on the porch. The bayou conveys its messages in the dead of night. We'll let the swamp decide."

The room grew colder. He tried to listen for her breathing, but he could hear only the sounds of the night. He turned toward the door, still open.

"Well, either she's dead or asleep," he said. "Will you be okay out on the porch?"

Delphine moved out of the doorway and let the screen door slam. "If I could brave the wild animals, I'd sleep in the forest. Anything to be away from that old hag. The porch will have to do. Remember, nothing you see in your dreams is real."

~

LINCOLN DIDN'T REMEMBER FALLING asleep. The most disturbing part of his dream was that he knew exactly where he was, in the witch's lair, and exactly what he was doing, sleeping. Such a revelation would normally wake him up, yet he remained at that level of unconsciousness like a fisherman who'd dozed off in his boat—pole still in hand— waiting for a bite.

A bird was whistling outside the open window. As he focused on the song, he realized it wasn't a bird at all. He turned to his side and saw a young man decked out in a Confederate uniform, whittling on a stick and whistling "Dixie" as he rocked in the creaky chair. The boy couldn't have been older than twenty.

"Have you come to haunt my dreams?" Lincoln thought if that was the best the swamp witch could conjure, the night was bound to be long and tedious.

The boy pointed the sharpened piece of wood at him. "I've just got one question. Who in the name of Jefferson Davis named you Lincoln?"

That wasn't the first time he'd been harassed for the culturally insensitive name. "That would be my mother. She expected me to go into politics and thought the name would soften the image of me being a Southerner. I went by Colin for most of my school years, but inevitably, someone would figure out my real name. Eventually, I decided to embrace it."

The youth shrugged. "I guess we've all got crosses to bear." He returned to his work on sharpening the stick.

"I don't mean to be rude, but what are you doing here?"

"You wanted to see me, so here I am."

Lincoln nodded. "You're Anthony Laurette." *Which means I'm not you reincarnated.*

"Right on both counts."

He found sitting up hard in spite of the fact that only his spirit moved. His body was still lying on the bed. "You can hear my thoughts?"

The young man grimaced at him. "What exactly do you think we're doing here? Your thoughts are all I hear. You are not some reincarnation. Each time the bucket of life gets dipped in the *deep waters,* it comes up with a fresh soul. It's made up of a bunch of other souls, to be sure, but it's uniquely itself. Understand?"

The initial question of his identity wasn't his real reason for having made the journey. "I need to know how to control your father, the baron Malveaux."

"Then you want in on the curse?"

He'd never considered that the family curse somehow controlled the baron in the afterlife. "Explain."

"He thinks he's in charge of the afterlife—or did until he was captured." The boy used the stick as if pointing at different realities. "As the living have to pass through Guinee to reach the *deep waters* upon their death, there wasn't a lot that could be done from your side to influence him. Think of him as guarding the gate. But he stole that power from the loas of the dead, so there was a mutual desire among both the living and those in charge of Guinee to rein in Baron Malveaux. In life, the curse was meant to harm the old man by threatening his heirs. That threat worked like a leash holding back an ill-behaved dog. You moved him out of the gate, but he's still not tamed."

"And the swamp witch is the one holding the other end of the leash?" Lincoln's heart beat faster at the idea of exerting that level of control.

"It's not that simple. Some things don't translate well from my reality to yours. If you want a say in how that leash is used, you'll have to lose your soul to the curse. Basically, you'll become part of the leash. That's the price."

Even if the old swamp witch held the curse in her hands, being a part of the spell had to give him powers over the baron that she couldn't control. "And if I sell my soul, I'll have complete control over the baron?"

"You know, even when I was alive, I found people's greed and lust for power perplexing. You think of evil as some attack dog that will sit calmly beside your chair until the command to attack is given. The witch is right. You are a fool."

"All animals can be trained."

The soldier took off his cap and revealed deep wrinkles around his eyes. "We're talking about someone who, in life, found a way to steal power from the gods. In death, he was able to keep them at bay even though outnumbered. He's wild but cunning. This is not an adversary you'll be able to defeat. A leash has a purpose, but the one holding the end is the one in command."

The thought that Baron Malveaux had stolen his power made Lincoln all the more determined. The baron was an opponent worthy of Lincoln's life lessons. If he were to win that battle, the resulting power might finally satiate his unrequited desire.

"What do I need to do?" Lincoln asked.

"Once Kendell Summer opened the curse, she made it accessible by members of the direct family. It's a two-sided coin. Those most in danger from the curse are also those who can enter the stream of dark energy."

He knew someone must have been designated to prevent exactly what he had in mind. "What about the swamp witch?"

"She's the guardian, but she's not of our lineage. Cross her, and she'll let loose hell on you, but she can't enter the nether regions. You can. Just know once you combine with the curse, there's no turning back. You'll be in a lifelong struggle to make the mad dog behave. An uncontrolled attack animal can easily turn on its master—or chew through its lead."

For someone who had spent his life in opposition to his father and sought to protect his heirs from the curse, Anthony Laurette was surprisingly accepting of Lincoln taking charge.

"And what about you?" Lincoln asked. "Will I be spending eternity with you as my adversary?"

The soldier began fading in the pale light. "I no longer exist."

In his place sat the old witch. "I summoned him from the dead to give you answers. Though I can see your future, I can't stop you. My time on Earth is nearing its end. A new generation will take up the battle."

"I have no intention of releasing the baron, if that's what you're worried about."

"I worry you won't know which side of the leash you're on. Close your eyes, and you'll enter the curse. Survive until morning, and I'll let you off the island. Should you become the rabid dog, though, I'll put you down."

He didn't doubt she had the power to carry out her threat, but her days were numbered. "I have no intention of being possessed. He'll find the leash is attached to a choke collar."

"Brave words."

The room faded to black, and nightmares filled his mind —deaths from the curse in vivid, emotional detail with him as both the victim and the villain. He experienced every life that had been tortured by the baron's deeds—from the women he'd forced into prostitution, to Anthony's sister Serephine as the pipe tool slit her delicate young wrist, all the way to Marilyn Fontenot, who died recently on that parade float. The fear experienced by the victims, however, paled in comparison to the adrenaline-filled rush of excitement as the curse fulfilled its destiny.

By morning, he understood what the witch had meant by getting lost in the connection of the curse to the baron. A rabid dog sought only to kill, and he'd tasted of that bloodlust. A wild animal, however, lacked control. The curse wasn't the source of power, but it would hold him to the baron. The untamed aggression they shared would unite them in a common cause.

He stumbled from the cot and made his way to the living room. "I'm still human."

Everything had been a dream.

The witch hadn't moved from her chair. "That is yet to be seen."

BACK IN HIS OFFICE, Lincoln paced around the crudely carved voodoo fetish like a cat stalking his prey. Since he had gained control, he needed to figure out how to release the trapped spirit. The anticipation of finally commanding so much aggression mixed with his anxiety of the unknown.

He sat in his office chair and stared the figure in the face. What he *should* do was call Delphine for a consultation. She'd secured the baron, so she would surely know how to release him. Doing so would probably involve some incantation and stinking up his office with perfume. Knowing the old goat, Lincoln figured a sacrificial virgin might even be involved.

Trusting Delphine, however, had never given him exactly what he'd wanted. Like all her ancestors before her, she had an unnerving habit of mixing in some personal vendetta, escape clause, or stipulation into her voodoo spells. The last thing he wanted was someone else tugging at the leash. *This is between me and you,* mon pere. He tapped his fingers on his glass desk to ease his need for action.

Light from his office's floor-to-ceiling windows reflected off the antique blue glass bottle nestled in a fur-and-leather-lined cavity in the belly of the statue. A thick dark liquid filled half of the square container. He knew what he had to do. Controlling the baron would only be another frustrating rung up the ladder. He wanted the power himself, not just to control it. *You stole from the gods. That's the kind of supremacy I seek.*

Before he had time to think about what he was doing, he plunged his hand into the hole and wrested the jar out of the belly of the voodoo doll. As he removed the bottle, prickly needles that felt as if they were from a miniature porcupine lodged in his skin, but the liquid fully occupied his attention. He used his fingernails to peel the wax-sealed cap off the top. The smell of death from the small opening filled his nose as if the liquid was trying to reach out and pull him in. *I haven't come all this way to stop now.* He lifted the bottle to his lips and upended it into his mouth, draining it in one shot.

The stuff tasted like tar thinned with rum. As it spread down his throat like molasses, the acidic vapor filled his nose and sinuses. Even his ears felt as though the viscous fluid was backing up into his Eustachian tubes. His eyes burned. He tossed the empty bottle onto his desk and grabbed the arms of his chair. His natural bodily reaction was to vomit the vile substance from his stomach, but his inner control kept him in his seat. He was headed for death or omnipotent power—no turning back.

The feeling of black death spreading down his throat didn't stop at his stomach. A chill radiated out from his heart as if it were pumping liquid nitrogen instead of blood. He leaned back in his chair, certain he was facing the end of his life. *Hopefully, this stuff only kills and doesn't turn me into a zombie.*

"You should be so lucky." The voice he heard was his, but deeper and darker. It reminded him of the fluid he'd consumed.

Lincoln knew it was the baron, but instead of carrying on a conversation with him, the banker's memories from the 1800s intermixed with Lincoln's. Once he had the man's life melded with his, the spirit's observations from watching the living for a hundred and fifty years in Guinee revealed themselves. Lincoln struggled to maintain a sense of identity as he was overcome by a multitude of thoughts and memories that were becoming his own. *I am my own leash.* The baron would become a part of him, not the other way around.

His human brain could only hold so much information, though. Like a computer that had been tasked with too many simultaneous processes, he sat frozen in his chair, unable to form a coherent thought. In desperation, he closed his eyes and hoped for sleep.

~

BY THE TIME the morning sun crept over the river and lit up his office, Lincoln Laroque had absorbed a life that had spread over two hundred years. His mind had rebooted. The baron Malveaux was no more, but every thought, memory, and accomplishment was now an integral part of Lincoln—as were all of the evil spirit's lusts and powers.

Having the memories and understanding them, however, were two very different things. His right palm itched. Though it had been the hand he'd thrust into the statue, the tiny thorns had covered the back of his hand, not the palm. No matter what he grabbed, the irritation wouldn't abate. Something was missing. He had to get up and move. Sitting behind a desk all day wasn't the way to live.

He passed his secretary as he left his office. "I'm going to Gottlieb's. I need some new suits. This thing feels like it's made of burlap."

"Didn't you just buy that one last week? I can call Brooks Brothers. They have your measurements on file."

Was I ever so naïve? "Not this time." A new suit wasn't just about the attire. It took an old-style haberdasher who understood his trade to properly fit a gentleman of means, and a man of power had to look the part. Being at the top of the business world had meant the most expensive, but traditional, suit he could find. As a peer of the gods, he needed something that would stand out. *Then I've got a score to settle.*

Walking helped calm his nerves and settle the old

memories in with the new. Each street he saw, along with every building he passed, developed a personal history within his mind, stretching back through the two hundred years of his shared consciousness. The nagging sensation that something was missing, however, only increased with each step. His hand tingled as though he'd slept on it. Flexing and shaking to get the blood moving, however, did nothing to alleviate the feeling of pins and needles jabbing his fingers.

From his experience possessing Myles's body, he knew the old tailor at Gottlieb's could whip up a suit with only a moment's notice, provided enough cash was involved in the transaction. At the time, he had insisted on the long coats of a bygone area and fashionably colorful vests, and the establishment had found it profitable to bow to his whims of fashion. A well-appointed section of the haberdashery looked equal parts steampunk gallery and museum. The combination worked perfectly for his desires.

The tailor was at his side the moment he started inspecting the silk linings. "These aren't just reproductions of a past age. We custom designed them to be light enough to fit comfortably even in the heat of summer."

Of course, the man didn't recognize Lincoln. The baron had possessed Myles's body when last they'd met.

"I'm seeking a unique look," Lincoln said. "It's not to be a costume but something I could wear every day. Suddenly, normalcy has grown boring to me."

"I understand completely, sir. Top hat and tails but with an eye toward modern comfort more than the avant-garde."

The differing aspects of Lincoln were finding their place

in his new reality. "I'd like some specially monogrammed items as well. Put your designer on creating a calligraphic *CM* for Colin Malveaux, with skulls ornamenting the three angles of the M."

The name fit. Condensing Lincoln to something less Yankee and reclaiming his birthright mixed the two versions of what he knew of himself, but something was still missing.

The old man fitted the last of the accoutrements to the new suit. "Colin" turned toward the mirror to inspect each aspect of the new attire. The powerful businessman would be laughed out of any boardroom in the silky black garment with blood-red lining and accessories. "I'm still missing something."

"The leather top hat is being sized. It will be ready momentarily. How would you like this order billed?"

"I'll be opening a new account. Put it under Colin Malveaux."

As he left the shop, he kicked the threshold and nearly fell. Instinctively, he tried to plant his walking stick for stability. It wasn't in his hand. *I need that cane!*

A sense of panic swept through him such as he'd never experienced. Emotional control had been his hallmark in business. The sudden feeling came from his newfound memories. He leaned against the doorframe and closed his eyes to retrieve the source of his apprehension. A single word dominated his thoughts: *power.*

Despite his owning all the baron's old memories, some were buried so deep he had to approach them with care. Whatever he'd done as Baron Malveaux was carefully hidden from anyone who might probe his thoughts, and that included the new owner of that history.

Source of power.

The additional words illuminated what was really missing. Somehow, the walking stick had connected him to the beyond—to the loa from whom he'd stolen his power. In the rush of so many memories, he'd lost track of his ultimate desire. *But where is that damn cane?* He traced back through the memories of his mother handing over the black stick with the silver-skull handle in the bank. The feeling of being completely back among the living with the cane in his hand left him all the more desperate to find it.

Those damn kids! He'd been abducted. When they'd taken the burlap sack off his head on the far side of the river, the cane was missing. He needed to find those responsible for his kidnapping. In all likelihood, they didn't even know what they'd stolen.

As much as he wanted revenge for having been removed from that idiot Myles and imprisoned in the voodoo fetish, that retaliation would have to wait. They were his only link to what had happened to his cane. Without that mystical stick, he was no more than a repository of useless history. He'd also find it pointless to confront his family without proof of his claim to the proverbial throne.

Conflicting emotions vied for dominance when he thought about confronting Kendell. As Baron Malveaux, he'd suffered her success at removing him from her boyfriend, but even that misogynistic side of him admired her strength and resilience. No matter what had been thrown at her—kidnapping her dog, abducting her friends, even possessing her boyfriend—she'd found a way to strike back. As Lincoln Laroque, he'd played with her like a cat toying with a mouse. He'd first threatened those she loved then offered her and her band musical fame and fortune to gain her cooperation.

His age-old natural desire for conflict confronted his modern education as he considered turning an enemy into an ally. The question was which option would work best on the bohemian young woman. Though bedding her would fulfill the threat he'd made to Myles, Colin feared giving in to the baron's lust for aggressive sexual domination might make him emotionally vulnerable. Whether she ended up an adversary or ally, that moron of a boyfriend would have to go.

5

_M_yles's considered opinion about all the dead people who kept showing up was that the only reasonable response was to get blind, stinking drunk. Not a single member of the recently dead had passed from natural causes—stabbed, shot, drugged, beaten, hit with a car, or fallen off a motorcycle. He was beginning to feel that mass murderer might be his next career move. He was certainly learning the moves from the victim's perspective.

Also, the loas of the dead weren't any help. Though he kept showing up at the gates of the cemeteries with the recently dead, like some Uber hearse driver for the soul, not a single guardian stuck around long enough to explain his latest predicament.

He poured another glass from a half-empty bottle of Captain Morgan. Typically, he preferred mixed drinks, but being alone in his apartment wasn't a party. His goal was complete intoxication, and the faster, the better. After midnight on a hot, humid Friday in summer, the dead showed up like traveling bands of Jehovah's witnesses. Unfortunately, not one of them had the good manners to wait at the door. At least then, he could ignore them. Maybe his being drunk would convince the unfortunate souls that he wasn't their best choice in spiritual transportation.

"Feeling a little sorry for yourself, don't you think?"

Myles looked up to see Papa Ghede pushing a glass across the table toward the bottle of rum. The diminutive original conveyor of the dead to the afterlife wore his traditional dusty top hat and tails along with his ever-annoying smile.

Myles did his best not to slur his words. "You've got some explaining to do."

"Did you really think all that travel back and forth to the *deep waters* wouldn't have some lasting effect on your life? The living don't see the underlying truth, but you do. Once a person dies, they're no longer distracted by life's experiences. All their senses—sight, smell, touch, hearing, taste—along with earthly desires and daily emotions are all washed away. Ask yourself, what's a person left with?"

He wanted to toss the glass at the first human who'd ever died. "You know damn well that's how I access the other side. I focus on what I am when everything I know about life is removed. All I'm left with is the realization I'm not a separate being but actually a part of every other living thing."

Papa Ghede stopped waiting for Myles to pour the drink and did the honors himself. "That's why the recently dead find you. Everyone else is busy focusing on their own lives.

You are *aware*. Plus, you're an associate of the loas of the dead. That makes you our natural go-between."

"I'm pretty positive I didn't ask for the job. You can't just go around making people do what you want."

The man's smile never left his face. "I can, actually, but for the most part, I choose not to. Did you really think that time you spent in Guinee talking to all the other loas was just about getting you out from the baron's possession? They were interviewing you. If you really didn't want to be one of us, you shouldn't have made all those trips to our domain. A member of the living stopping by the land of the dead doesn't go unnoticed, and someone like you, who can make the trip so effortlessly, piques our interest. Still, we would have left you alone had you not started bringing people with you. I'm afraid this is really all your doing, my friend."

Myles downed another shot of rum. The old man's words rang a little too true. Even when he had tried to prove to Kendell that he wasn't imagining things, he knew he was, in part, showing off. Nothing good ever came from being arrogant.

"Then at least tell me what the job of loa of the dead entails," Myles said. "I seem to have missed my orientation."

The man's smile burst into a full-throated laugh. "I've spent two hundred thousand years in Guinee. The other loas aren't as experienced as I, but each of them has paid their dues. You'll be more like our errand boy. Consider it a promotion from greeter to the dead. From time to time, there will be favors we'll ask of you. Being a part of the living makes you more fit for some of the chores that come along with accepting a newly dead person."

"If I agree to help, will you stop the recently deceased from showing up at all hours and all places? I feel like I'm losing my mind. In case you didn't know, it's not natural for people with gunshot wounds to just stroll up to someone and ask to be escorted to a cemetery."

Papa Ghede set his glass next to the bottle. "If that's what it takes, we have a deal. No more dead spirits looking for guidance. You'll only see them if we've agreed on our side that you can help and we can't."

"I could still use a little guidance. After all, if you're sending me on a mission you can't accomplish yourself, it's probably not as simple as pouring drinks at the bar."

He nodded toward the bottle. "Get a better brand of rum. That one's not fit for a proper loa of the dead. Anytime you need to talk, pull it out, and pour two drinks. One of us will find our way to you."

Myles's drunken fog made conducting an informed negotiation hard. "Would it be too rude to ask what's in it for me? So far, this arrangement sounds more like extortion."

"Payment will be commensurate with the task. Remember, you created this problem. Many in Guinee would be happier to see you pass on to the *deep waters* permanently. We guard the gates. You coming and going as you please is like an unruly schoolboy who jumps fences just for the fun of it. By repeatedly trespassing into our domain, you've shown others they might be able to neglect our position as guardians as well. What I'm offering you is legitimacy, kind of like how a police detective might hire a criminal."

Myles had never considered how his flights of psychometry might not be looked on favorably by spirits from the other side. "So if I help you, I can continue to visit the reservoir of humanity without opening a breach between the living and the dead?"

"We'll provide you cover, but only if you work with us instead of doing as you please. Do we have a deal?"

He couldn't imagine *not* taking his trips into the unknown as that connection to all life had gotten him through some hard times. "Fine. I'll do it."

"Good. Because I have a job for you. Somewhere in New Orleans is a black walking stick that belonged to Archibald Malveaux. It originally belonged to Baron Samedi and was the source of Malveaux's power over the seventh gate of Guinee. I'd like the cane returned."

Myles did his best to focus on Papa Ghede in the hopes that his mind might follow his eyes' lead. "How did Malveaux steal an item from Guinee?"

The old man squirmed in the chair. "Well, that's not one of our prouder moments. But as you're our assistant and confidant, knowing the story might help in your search. On February 24, 1857, New Orleans had its first Mardi Gras parade. Baron Samedi thought the loas of the dead should be represented at such an auspicious event. Archibald Malveaux was already the city's most powerful banker. So of course, he financed much of the celebration."

Myles could almost envision the scene. "And of course, a

baron of Guinee would expect to ride on the main float, as would the one putting up the money."

"How Malveaux managed to steal the cane isn't clear, but you can at least see how the two came into contact. Ever since that first parade, by law, every member of every float must wear a mask. This was instituted by Malveaux to prevent Samedi from finding him. The beads tossed from the floats were Samedi's response. They're meant to be offerings from the dead to the living for the return of the walking stick."

Myles wanted another drink, but he needed what few faculties he had left. "So that's how Baron Malveaux maintained his control over the seventh gate, but we imprisoned that asshole."

"Exactly. While Malveaux was a baron of Guinee, we didn't dare make a move against him. He'd stashed the cane somewhere in the New Orleans Bank and Trust as his symbol of control. Now that he's gone from Guinee, his walking stick is missing."

No wonder that pain in the ass kept hold of that damn stick. "After Baron Malveaux took possession of me, the head of the bank handed him the cane. It was never farther away than he could reach. I thought he just used it to intimidate people."

"Do you remember what happened to it?"

"No, but I have some ideas on where to start."

MYLES WOKE up the next day, slumped over the small table,

the empty bottle of Captain Morgan lying near his head. *Couldn't you have at least prevented the hangover?* He figured Papa Ghede had better things to do than look after his newly hired lackey, though.

The sound of the Keurig spitting out hot coffee made him raise his head toward the kitchen. Even in his haze, he could make out Kendell in her work attire. "Hey." The word exhausted his ability to force air through his voice box.

"Charlie warned me you'd headed home from the bar with a bottle in hand last night. I thought you might need some coffee and maybe a friendly face to wake up to." She replaced the empty bottle with the steaming cup. "Feel like talking about what's going on? I know I pushed you awfully hard to introduce me to Robert Johnson, but I've never seen you turn to alcohol after a psychometric trip."

"It's not that." He couldn't be completely sure that the last journey hadn't pushed the loas over the edge, though. "Escorting the recently dead to the gates of Guinee has become something of a second job. Last night, Papa Ghede finally turned up to answer some questions. Guess I've been promoted from guide to servant for the loas of the dead."

She stared into her coffee. "You know, to anyone else, that would sound really strange. I've been messing around with voodoo too. I'm no assistant loa of the dead, not even a voodoo queen, but I'd like to help. We've always made pretty good partners."

Her working with him might keep him in the loop of what she had planned, at least. Anything would beat having to rush to her aid without a clue about the nature of the danger.

"No argument there," he said. "I could use the help. He's already given me my first assignment. I need to find that walking cane Baron Malveaux had with him. Apparently, it's how he maintained his position as guardian of the seventh gate. He stole it from Baron Samedi. When your homeless friends kidnapped me, him, whatever… the cane got lost in the scuffle."

"So we've got another magical object loose on the streets. Where should we start?"

That question had dominated every halfway sober waking moment of the previous restless night. "Even with you as the guardian angel of the homeless, approaching them directly seems like a way of broadcasting our search to every nefarious fortune hunter in the city. If they did take it —and we're lucky—the cane will probably pop up in one of the expensive pawn shops. If someone is holding onto it, it'd be worth talking to Lieutenant Cazenave. He'd be the one to hear of any street brawl involving a malevolent walking cane. Beyond that, I can only come up with Madam de Galpion. I can't see her taking it, but maybe she can explain how Archibald Malveaux learned about the cane in the first place."

"You think Marie Laveau somehow helped Malveaux steal the cane?"

Myles didn't know what to think. "It's not like Malveaux would have known where to find Baron Samedi. Even when the two did meet, I can't see how a human could steal a loa of the dead's possession without some paranormal help. I know you consider Delphine a friend, but she shares her ancestor's peculiar ideas about loyalty."

Bringing up Delphine often resulted in a disagreement. Kendell looked back at the empty bottle before responding. "Fair enough, but give me a logical argument about why you think Marie Laveau was working for Archibald Malveaux— not just your suspicions. She did cast the curse against him."

The coffee helped Myles focus on Kendell, who'd apparently stopped rocking side to side in the chair opposite him. "I keep coming back to Luther Noire's hint that Marie had worked for Archibald. Casting the curse against Malveaux's heirs was a drastic move for his business sins."

He could see Kendell's irritation building. She never responded well to her ancestor's treatment of women.

"Not that what he did to women wasn't evil," Myles continued. "I'm just saying the curse wasn't so much aimed at him as those who came after him. Delphine talks a lot about a spell needing balance. Maybe this one was Marie's way of evening the situation for helping him take the cane. The cane gave Baron Malveaux power in the afterlife. The curse takes aim at his descendants who pass through his gate as a constant reminder of what he'd done."

Kendell shivered in spite of the warm, humid morning. "We're coming back around to that curse again. I really thought we'd finished with it."

He knew she felt a familial responsibility. "You can't escape your history. The baron Malveaux was every bit as much your ancestor as Louis Broussard, who commissioned the spell."

"I feel like the little Dutch girl with her finger in the dike."

He wondered if that made him the hydrological engineer who'd come to direct the flow in her metaphor. "Us being partners is as much about supporting each other as finding answers."

She reached for his hand. "And lovers?"

In spite of his hangover, he leaned in and kissed her. "That transcends our earthly obligations."

~

MYLES FINISHED WIPING down the bar and ducked into the back room for the mop, to start working on the cement floor.

After the front door slammed shut, Charlie irately said, "We're closed, officers."

Papa Ghede had managed to convince the recently dead to give Myles a break, but unfortunately, his influence didn't extend to the police.

"Is there a Myles Garrison that works here?" someone asked. "We'd like to have a word with him."

Myles darted out of the utility closet and grabbed Charlie's arm before he did something stupid. "I'm Myles," he told the two uniformed officers. "What can I do for you?"

"We need you to come down to the station and answer some questions."

As lead bartender, Charlie never let Myles step into the line of fire alone. "What's he being charged with?"

"Nothing as yet. We'd just like to have a chat."

Myles didn't like being hauled in to the police station in the dead of night, but going voluntarily meant Charlie wouldn't do something so drastic that they'd both be looking for outside help. "It's okay, Charlie. I'm sure it's nothing."

Charlie didn't turn his head away from the police even though he addressed Myles. "Do you want me to notify Kendell?"

"Not yet. If you don't hear from me by morning, round up the troops."

"I don't like the idea of you going to the station alone. It's awfully late for a *chat*."

Myles untied the cleaning apron and handed it to Charlie. "I just hate making you finish up for me."

Out on the street with the two silent, burly cops, Myles wasn't quite so confident. "Can you at least tell me what this is about?"

"The chief will fill you in soon enough."

He wondered if running would be such a bad idea. He hadn't been charged with anything. Had Lieutenant Cazenave been the one wanting to talk, Myles would have gone happily, but Chief of Police Laroque wasn't a person he had any interest in meeting—especially not at two in the morning in what was sure to be a mostly empty police station. "Charlie has a lot of contacts around the city, including a number of reporters."

They turned off Bourbon Street toward the towering marble station. "You're just being questioned. No need to get paranoid."

Myles was having trouble *not* envisioning every negative outcome as he was escorted into the station occupied by only the night crew. His two companions obviously had no information regarding his plight. They didn't seem the type someone in charge was likely to confide in. After the obligatory paperwork, he was left in an interrogation room that could have been used for a Hollywood location shoot. It looked straight out of some crime drama, with its lime-green tiled walls, one-way mirror, and corner surveillance cameras.

He sat at a metal table, more annoyed than concerned. From his time bingeing cop shows, he knew the time alone was supposed to make him feel vulnerable. With his connection to the loas of the dead, it did the opposite. Though he didn't have a hip flask of rum to call one forth, in his isolation and intense emotional state, he could tell they weren't far off.

In spite of his renewed bravado, he jerked in the chair when the heavy door opened. Chief of Police Gerald Laroque wasn't a hard man to mistake, with his linebacker build, military-cut gray hair, and steely-blue eyes. "I'll start by apologizing for the theatrics. I'm sure my men gave you a bit of a scare hauling you in so late at night. This is the only place in the city I knew we could talk without being overheard."

Myles breathed a little more easily. Fear number one—of being roughed up in a room where no one would be watching—had been alleviated. That left only another hundred or so possibilities. "What's this about?"

The big man sat in the chair opposite Myles. "I understand from Lieutenant Cazenave that you know my nephew, Lincoln. I believe you've also had some experience with my ancestor, Archibald Malveaux."

Myles was not likely to forget one or the other. "I can't say either has been an enjoyable encounter."

"I would guess not. My nephew has done something rather foolish. He's bonded with the spirit of our ancestor."

Myles had to hand it to the chief. He had a way of dramatically presenting his situation with few words. Despite being sure they weren't being overheard, Myles leaned across the table and nearly whispered, "He's been possessed?"

"Unfortunately, no. Unlike what you endured, Lincoln has voluntarily joined his spirit with Archibald's. They are no longer two separate individuals. He's calling himself Colin Malveaux."

Once the danger of having been summoned to the station passed, Myles noticed the deep lines around the chief's eyes and across his forehead. "I was led to believe by Lieutenant Cazenave that you didn't believe in the paranormal."

"Joe is a good man. I hated firing him."

Myles's heart felt as if it had come to a full stop. "What?"

"It's not what you think. I run law enforcement in the city, and my men respect me. But that doesn't mean there aren't spies in my department. My family excels at having secret tendrils even in our own organizations. With Colin attempting to gather all the reins in his hands, I needed to keep Joe's activities out of the police protocol. I called you in here tonight in such a way that if anyone is watching, you'll appear to be someone I distrust. Firing Joe gives him the freedom *not* to follow the department's rules. I could have let him make contact with you on his own, but I wanted you to hear it from me first. Colin Malveaux is a threat to the peace and safety of this city and, I fear, to much more than that."

Myles wasn't sure how far to trust the police chief. "I'm just a bartender. What are you asking me to do?"

Gerald Laroque's fingers looked like miniature boudin sausages as he slid a slip sealed envelope across the table. "You are one of the few people who've successfully stood up to Archibald Malveaux. Meet with Joe. That's all I ask. From there, the less I know, the better."

6

*M*yles was still on edge from meeting the police chief when he quietly entered Kendell's apartment. At five in the morning, his previous day still hadn't ended, but her day was about to start.

As he closed the door, Cheesecake stretched her front legs in greeting. At least she hadn't barked.

"We're making progress aren't we, girl?" he asked.

The pup gave him a low growl as her answer. He might be welcome, but his timing was somewhat suspicious.

Though he sneaked into Kendell's bedroom, hoping not to wake her, she was already propped up against the pillows. "You're late. Out carousing with another dead woman?"

He sat next to her and pulled out the open envelope. "I wish. Chief of Police Laroque and I had a little chat."

Her eyes opened so wide he suspected she wouldn't need coffee to get her day started until after she got to work. "At least you're not in jail. What did he want?"

He waved the folded page at her. "The baron is up to his old tricks. This time, though, he's using the body of Lincoln Laroque. This letter is from Joe Cazenave. He's asking for a meeting. I can bring whomever I want so long as they're willing to delve into another adventure regarding the curse. His one exception is Delphine de Galpion."

Kendell took the paper from him. "Why on earth would she be excluded?"

"He doesn't say, but from the location of the meeting, I have to guess Luther Noire will be involved."

The note wasn't that long, but based on how Kendell studied it, he had to believe she was trying to read between the lines.

"Who should we bring?" she asked.

He smiled, realizing she'd immediately made herself a coconspirator. "I still think Professor Yates is more con man than scientist, but if we're dealing with paranormal objects again, I'll want his input."

"He won you over with his little contraptions, didn't he?"

The college class he'd shared with Kendell seemed like a lifetime ago. If not for the professor's wild ideas, Myles might have been out scouring the desert for artifacts like any normal archeology grad student. "He helped save the band—and me."

She bit her lip as she looked at him. "I'll want Polly and the girls with me."

Polly Urethane and the Strippers had been the first ones Myles had called when Kendell had put herself in danger. Their involvement led to their kidnapping. Putting the women at risk again conflicted with Myles's inherent chivalry.

"Don't you think they've done enough already?" he asked.

"Polly would pull my amp wires if I don't include her. At least let the band members come to the meeting and let them decide. I couldn't have rescued you from the baron without them."

Events had been pretty hazy while he was under the baron's possession. He remembered the band playing on the improvised stage while he endured the exorcism, but beyond that, he didn't know how much the girls knew about the paranormal activities of their lead guitarist. "With the four of them, Professor Yates, you, and me, that'll be seven of us. Luther's office isn't that big."

She wrapped her arms around him like a little girl who didn't want to get up and go to school. "I trust my bandmates with my life and, more than that, with yours and Cheesecake's. If they come along, then we won't have to rehash the conversation to them only to have Polly ask us questions we should have thought of at the meeting. One way or another, you know they're going to be involved."

∽

THE PARKING GARAGE under Harrah's casino was easy enough to slip into undetected. Myles hoped the diverse group—the band members, Professor Yates, Kendell, and himself—would blend in well enough with the tourists searching for their cars.

Kendell kept hold of his hand. "Why couldn't we just walk up to the front door like last time?"

He knew Luther Noire was getting a little prickly at all the activity around the supposedly abandoned World Trade Center. "There's too many of us. It'd look suspicious. Lieutenant Cazenave says there's an access down here to the building's basement. Something about a tunnel that was meant as a way to divert traffic that got sealed off. He said Harrah's has been using it for overflow parking."

Designed as a multilane thoroughfare, the tunnel wasn't hard to find. Sneaking past the valets took only a bit of stealth. The door to the World Trade Center had been sealed shut for decades, and Myles was certain Mr. Noire had done his best to retain the nonoperational look of the heavy metal hatch just as he had the building itself. Fortunately, that was all an illusion. As they approached, the door opened without a sound, though Myles was certain an alarm was going off in the portly man's office to confirm what the cameras were capturing.

Lieutenant Cazenave ushered them in and checked the empty makeshift parking garage to make sure they hadn't been observed. "Head past the pump station. There's an elevator on the other side."

For being in a building with supposedly only one tenant, the basement machinery was actively keeping the tower's environment well controlled.

The maintenance elevator easily accommodated all nine people.

Lieutenant Cazenave pulled the heavy gate down with a loud slam. "From here on, it'd be best if you just called me

Joe. I can't risk having any ties to the police department." With his discreetly muscular build and precise movements, though, he'd never be mistaken as anything other than law enforcement, military, or spy.

The elevator's control panel had been removed, leaving only a cluster of bare wires. The cage ascended on its own. Myles expected it to stop on the twenty-fourth floor and Luther's office, but as it continued upward, he felt a little like Charlie in the chocolate factory, wondering if the lift was ever going to stop. He looked up through the nonexistent ceiling of the freight elevator at the top of the building. "Where are we meeting Luther?"

Joe's look of unconcern didn't ease Myles's apprehension. The man probably wouldn't show fear in the middle of a hurricane. "With a group this large, Luther likes conducting meetings in the old restaurant on the top floor. It has a wonderful three-hundred-sixty-degree view of the city."

Myles knew fear could be infectious, and the last thing he needed was the women getting jittery.

Kendell snuggled to his side and took his hand. "I suspect this feeling I have is from all the magical artifacts stashed away in this building, but coming here gives me the creeps."

He squeezed her hand as his way of appreciating her understanding. "I'm sure we're fine. Luther wants whatever we find. Joe may not work for him, but they clearly have a business arrangement. But I know what you mean. I'd have preferred to have this meeting in your apartment."

"I don't think Cheesecake would have appreciated so many people invading her space."

The elevator came to a halt with a bounce that nearly made Myles lose his balance. His earlier irrational fear had diminished slightly, but as the doors opened, four men in black combat fatigues appeared outside.

"What the hell?" Myles said.

Joe lifted the elevator gate. "Don't worry. These are my men. Whatever plan we come up with today will likely require some form of security. I trust these guys with my life and have had that trust confirmed on many occasions."

The circular room perched atop the thirty-three-story building had been cleared of all furniture except a lone conference table and chairs. The band members, including Kendell, headed for the windows encompassing the room.

"Can you imagine what this place must have been like?" she asked.

Polly leaned back against a window with a view of the river and pointed toward the stage. "That's the gig I'd have liked—rich old guys bringing their classy wives up here for an elegant meal while we jammed out some Runaways' classics. In our punk attire, we'd look like the snotty couples' illegitimate daughters. I can just see it."

Looking like a gentleman that might fit Polly's description, Luther came out of the kitchen wearing his seersucker suit. Behind him, his young secretary carried a plate of sandwiches.

"I'm afraid all I've got are muffulettas and cola," Luther said. "Please help yourself."

Lynn Seed turned away from the window with a

perplexed look as she stared at her phone. "How is it possible that there's no cell service up here? I wanted to send a picture of the view to Lars."

Luther helped his secretary arrange the table. "Not only won't you get any signal from outside this building, any pictures you take or recordings of any kind will automatically delete when you leave. That's why I set pads of paper and pens at every seat around the table. To keep all our little precious objects from doing harm, this building operates on a totally different energy wavelength."

Professor Yates took a seat near the head of the table, where Luther had set his notepad and lunch. "Fascinating. So that's what all the equipment was about in the basement?"

"A conversation for another time. I'm sure we'd have a lot to teach each other about strange energy signatures." Luther spread his hands, indicating everyone should take a seat. "Let's start off with what we know."

Kendell sat close to Myles. Clearly, she wasn't going to let the most obvious omission go without a fight. "Why isn't Delphine de Galpion here?"

"She's not here because I don't trust her," Luther said.

Myles wondered if being alone in such a large building had a way of reducing Luther's tact, or if it was the other way around.

"That's hardly a reason," Kendell said. "Without her help, I never would have saved Myles from Baron Malveaux. She knows more about Marie Laveau and her curses than anyone. We need her help."

A fight was brewing, and they hadn't even gotten around

to laying out the problem. Myles didn't trust Madam de Galpion any more than Luther, but calming Kendell was more important. Besides, she had a point.

"Madam de Galpion might be better approached in private," he said. "Once we know what we're doing, you can meet with her and figure out where she fits into the plan."

At least Kendell didn't turn her frustration on him. "I still don't like it. She has a right to defend herself."

"No one's made any accusations. In fact, no one's said anything. Maybe we should start with the problem at hand."

She settled back in her chair. "You're right. You met with Papa Ghede, so you should start."

"Lincoln Laroque and Baron Malveaux are now one person. He's calling himself Colin Malveaux, and he's after that walking cane he had when you guys saved me. When he had possession of me, I remember him being obsessed with that stick. It was never out of his reach. But I don't know what happened to it when you abducted me."

Minerva Wax looked up and down the table at everyone present. "Are you kidding me? We're all here to talk about some stupid cane?"

Even though the drummer for Polly Urethane and the Strippers wasn't the most militant feminist of the group, Kendell still had better rapport with her bandmate than Myles did. "The cane belonged to Baron Samedi. It was the source of Baron Malveaux's power in Guinee. We can't leave it loose on the streets."

Luther put down his sandwich. "That cane has a long history. Its power isn't isolated to the afterlife, but something prevented it from doing much damage in our reality. If Colin lays his hands on it, his next obsession will be to utilize its full potential. So the first question is what happened to it?"

Myles had woken Kendell up from numerous nightmares involving that day. He knew every moment of his kidnapping was indelibly imprinted in her memories.

"The homeless were keeping an eye on Myles while he was under the baron's possession," she said. "They did the kidnapping and delivered him to Whit, who brought Myles and Delphine across the river. The cane wasn't in the boat when Whit delivered Myles to the other side. I'd bet my guitar on it."

Polly nodded as if she'd hit on the answer. "So that means someone from the homeless community has it."

Myles could tell from the way Kendell tensed up that Polly had struck a nerve. "The homeless respect my family on the Westbank. They've been looking out for me. I can't believe they'd steal something."

"Maybe they considered it payment for abducting Myles. It's worth checking out." Polly was never very good at reading other's irritations.

Professor Yates scratched at the gray stubble on his chin. "Supposing that someone from the homeless community did get sticky fingers, it's not like them to hold onto something valuable. Being so commonplace, it would be a long shot for it to show up in one of the antique galleries on Royal, but I'll check with my contacts. I might also be able to modify my equipment to read the energy of something so powerful. If I can and I do pick up something, it'll take some triangulation to figure out the precise location. I guess my gypsy carnival trailer is going to start looking like a mobile CIA-inspired listening laboratory."

"We could check the junk shops along Decatur," Lynn said. "They're always on the lookout for cool steampunk-type items. I usually hit a couple of them a week just looking for new outfits. No one would notice a bunch of girls pawing through the new arrivals."

Kendell pulled the pad of paper from beside her plate and made some notes. "I'll go across the river and talk to my family. They'd know for sure if the cane was in the boat or not. And if not, they've got contacts among the homeless. If they are responsible, Mary will know. She can also vouch for Whit. I don't suspect that river rat. He's too invested in documenting the stories of the societies that live on the river to betray one, but it'll be good to cross him off the list."

Myles hated what he was about to say, but all suspects had to be accounted for. "Whit and I weren't the only people on that boat."

Kendell snapped around at him so quickly he flinched. "Not Delphine again. She was there to help you."

"I don't want to fight. I'm just trying to look at all options. You want to clear Whit. We should make sure Delphine is cleared, too."

Her voice softened slightly. "I'll meet with her. She wouldn't lie to me. Not about something so important as this."

Luther pointed at the glasses in Kendell's shirt pocket. "Bring those green lenses with you. They'll let you see the truth."

"Yes, sir." Her stoic response showed she'd been pushed too far.

Myles had never been much good at alleviating her anger, but he could dilute it. "Then there are the people sitting around this table. I know I didn't take it. Kendell wouldn't have a reason for wanting it. The two of us can vouch for the band members. None of them would have been in a position to take it, anyway. And Professor Yates wasn't involved in my capture. Though I doubt you'd personally perform the crime, Luther, an awful lot of paranormal objects end up in this building."

Every eye turned to the man at the head of the table. "You have a valid point. I wouldn't be hosting this meeting —and paying for Joe's protection contingent—if I didn't care what happened to that cane. It needs to be isolated from the living. No other artifact in my care comes close to being as potentially dangerous. But if I did have it, what reason would I have to deny it?"

Myles knew a potential conflict was brewing about who would eventually end up with the cane. "Your explanation still puts you on the list of those who'd like to end up with the magic stick."

"Rightly so," Luther said. "Let's consider that list for a moment. Colin Malveaux, of course, heads the group. We all know why he wants it. With all due respect to Kendell, the cane would make a nice addition to Delphine de Galpion's collection of books and things from Marie Laveau. Delphine's motivation for helping has to be seen in the light of her desire to own the cane. I do want to see an artifact from Guinee in my vault. I won't deny it. But ultimately, it isn't mine to possess. As the person with the closest ties to Guinee, Myles, can we expect any help from Baron Samedi? Or is he just going to sit back and wait until you deliver him his walking stick?"

Myles had never been much good at demanding an employer pull their own weight. "The loas of the dead are pretty clear that what happens in life is our business. As far as they are concerned, someone from life stole it, so it's up to the living to return it. Don't get me started about the affairs of the gods."

Polly kicked one high-heeled clear-plastic stripper shoe up to the lip of the table. "And what about you guys dressed in black? You just going to stand around looking menacing, or what?"

Joe spoke for his men. "There's a lot of chatter on the dark web about a reward for the cane. We'll chase down what we can and keep an eye on everyone performing physical searches. If you get into trouble, we'll be there before you know it."

Luther leaned forward conspiratorially. "We shouldn't meet like this again—only in small groups from now on. Don't trust anyone except those at this table. Even though Chief of Police Laroque might be sympathetic to our cause, you have to look on any cop as an adversary. Colin Malveaux and the Laroque family have enough money to hire an army of people to search this city, but a smart adversary would approach more as a friend than a foe."

~

RIDING the ferry across the river to the Westbank felt a little like visiting a favorite aunt that Kendell never quite found time to see. The outing made a good excuse to get Cheesecake out of the apartment. The pup pranced around the lower steel deck, allowing each passenger the privilege of patting her shaggy head.

As the boat churned across the Mississippi's current, Kendell peered downriver toward the cottonwood grove. Somewhere below the tree limbs and cooled by the breeze off the river, her extended family had their encampment. They no longer had to fight for their land, thanks to her, but she wasn't relying on their sense of obligation. They'd welcomed her into their hearts the moment Whit had brought her to their camp. She was one of them, and every member of the tribe looked out for each other unconditionally.

The aging ferry's engine revved up to combat the swift current before docking with a loud thud against the splintered wooden beams of the terminal. She held Cheesecake back as throngs of tourists disembarked and headed for the nearest bar. They didn't know what they were missing.

Up on the levee, a gentle breeze helped cool the oppressively hot and humid day. Despite Kendell having a mission, she enjoyed the leisurely walk. Mothers pushing strollers gave her cheerful greetings as they passed. Every child dropped to its knees to greet the dog on her own terms. Not only her extended family made the area feel inviting.

Something felt different about the neighborhood. The

brass plaques embedded in the walkway to explain the area's history had a renewed meaning for her. As far as she could see, that had been her ancestor's property. The main body of New Orleans had been the domain of Baron Malveaux, but his quiet hamlet had originally been the plantation of another great-great-great-grandfather, Louis Broussard—the one who'd lost everything, including his family, and commissioned the curse.

Cheesecake tugged at her leash, directing Kendell to the water fountain which had thoughtfully been designed with a spigot at doggy level.

"I know it's hot, girl."

As the hundred-year-old military compound came into view, they turned off the path and skidded down a concrete embankment to the river's batture. In the early afternoon, most of the conclave would be out panhandling on the streets, but the matriarch would be preparing lunch for any who hadn't been able to secure a meal.

Weaving through the tree trunks toward the open-pit fire felt a little like walking into her father's house after a year at college. She knew she was welcome but wondered if she should announce herself and the dog. The leaves rustled around them, and small twigs snapped under their feet. The noise was sufficient to rouse Mary from the pot of food she'd been hunched over.

"Kendell! My river angel, what are you doing here?" She rushed up and wrapped Kendell in her arms so tightly Kendell felt like a little girl being bear-hugged by her grandmother.

Cheesecake snuggled the older woman's leg.

"I wish this were just a social visit," Kendell said. "I really need to get over here more often. What are you cooking? It smells amazing."

Mary let her go and turned back to the pot on the fire. She ran her ladle through the thick broth, bringing up chunks of meat and roasted vegetables. Without asking, she layered two bowls of rice with the concoction and fished a meaty bone from the scraps for Cheesecake. "It's my version of étouffée. I have to use whatever's available, so it's never the same dish twice. Now, sit and tell me what I can do for you."

The food tasted every bit as good as it smelled.

"When Whit and Madam de Galpion brought Myles over in the skiff, did you happen to see a black walking cane with a silver skull handle?"

"No, but you're not the first to ask about it. Whit said some shady-looking characters were lurking around the camp after you left. He said the way they kept hidden in the brush reminded him of his military sniper training. Every time we tried to flush them out, they crept away like sneaky gators, but about a week after the exorcism party, one showed up in camp."

Kendell tried narrowing down the possibilities. If Baron Malveaux had had a security team, Myles would have known about it. The bank might have seen to the baron's protection, but a well-armed team wouldn't have sat back and let him be driven out of Myles. Chief of Police Laroque, however, might have been perfectly happy to see his ancestor contained and would have had the resources to know about the abduction. Finally, lurking in the shadows, was Luther Noire and his unending quest for paranormal items.

"What happened with your uninvited guest?"

"He threatened to start a legal battle over the deed you gave us if we didn't tell him about the cane. The whole thing stank worse than the riverbank at low ebb. We didn't know anything. I did, however, put feelers out to the homeless on both sides of the river—mostly for our protection. I like to know what's going on in case one of my people doesn't show up for dinner."

Kendell knew filing a missing person's report wouldn't do much good for the homeless. Crimes in the city had a way of being prioritized by the victim's economic status. The tribe had to fend for themselves. "Did you get any leads?"

"Nothing that made much sense, but then you're more in tune with the supernatural than I. The people who abducted your boyfriend said they did see the cane. They said the voodoo priestess took charge of it as your boyfriend was all tied up and Whit was busy piloting the boat. In all the confusion, she might have stashed the cane somewhere when they landed, but it's not here now, and none of us ever saw it. There's an additional story from a drunk who frequents the steps down to the river from the Quarter. He said she dumped it overboard during the crossing."

Kendell wasn't sure if that was good news or bad. "So it's lost to the river?"

"Here's where the story goes off the rails for me. According to him, he saw an alligator gar swallow the cane and swim upriver. It reminded me of an excuse Hawk would dream up for why he lost something. I'd keep looking for other explanations of where she might have hidden it if I were you."

Kendell had run across too many odd events to discount any possibility, but from what she knew about voodoo, enchanted sea creatures didn't fit that brand of magic. "But you do believe Delphine has the cane?" She feared she might have to admit to Myles that he'd been right all along.

Mary handed a piece of bread to Cheesecake to go with her bone. "From what I've gathered, it seems like whoever took it knew it was dangerous. Madam de Galpion might have taken it for safekeeping. If it's as desirable as it sounds, I'm happy it didn't end up with my people. And your boyfriend might have had a rougher time if that demon still had something magical to hold onto. Of all the potential thieves during the exorcism, I'd guess a voodoo priestess might not be the worst choice."

~

MYLES DIDN'T EXPECT Kendell to knock when she visited his apartment as she was a frequent enough visitor, but seeing Cheesecake standing at her side was a surprise. "This must be important if you brought the big dog."

She didn't seem in the mood for levity. "We were just across the river talking to Mary. I didn't know where else to go. It seems you may have been right about Delphine."

Myles had used up his lifetime supply of telling a woman *I told you so*. He'd only gotten to say it once and had lost a girlfriend for that momentary feeling of smug self-righteousness. "What do you propose we do?"

"I can't just bust in and demand the cane. I wouldn't know what to do with it if I had it. You said Baron Samedi would be able to take it back to Guinee once we find it. Before I go making an ass of myself—or worse, attracting attention to the cane's location—I need to know what's involved in returning him his walking stick."

Myles set three glasses on his kitchen table and proceeded to half fill them with twelve-year-old El Dorado rum. "Charlie swears by this stuff. Personally, I prefer a spiced rum for sipping, but I suspect the loas of the dead are more purists. With Cheesecake here, I wonder if I should include a shot in her doggy bowl just to honor her ancestors."

Kendell let the dog off her leash. "You know she's strictly a kibble-and-water girl. Dog treats are her only vice."

The old pooch jumped onto his worn couch and scratched out a comfortable place to lie down.

"She's always welcome here. I'm just not sure how she'll respond to a loa of the dead showing up out of thin air."

"Nothing about New Orleans's air in summer is *thin*. Couldn't you set your air conditioner to a reasonable temperature? This place oozes humidity."

"It's not his fault."

Myles turned toward the table. He'd met most of the loas of the dead during his possession by Baron Malveaux, but the tall dark man standing there with white skeleton markings wasn't one he remembered.

"You must be Baron Samedi," he said.

The man downed the rum in one swallow. "That I am. You have news about my walking stick?"

Myles was only able to drink half of the rum for courage. "We have a suspicion the descendant of Marie Laveau might have it. If we ask Madam de Galpion, though, we could alert Colin Malveaux. That is, if he hasn't already ransacked her shop."

The voodoo gentleman helped himself to another glass of rum. That one, he filled to the rim. "That old voodoo witch taught me not to drink rum without first seeing the sealed bottle, but I believe I can trust you. Her tainted libation is what put me in this predicament. It would make sense that her offspring would be the one to end up with my cane. Unfortunately, I dare not enter her domain uninvited. She has more of those voodoo fetish dolls. I'd hate to get stuck in one. I'll have to rely on you three to discover the truth."

Myles turned to Kendell and then Cheesecake. "I doubt the dog is going to be much use."

"My apologies. I only see her from the beyond. From my perspective, a hellhound can be quite convincing as a companion to a voodoo priestess."

Myles shook his head. "What voodoo priestess?"

"Why, your friend, of course. Do you really think we go handing out charmed golden gifts to just anyone? You three are on a magical journey together: you the assistant to the loas of the dead, Kendell the natural voodoo practitioner, and Cheesecake her vigilant protector."

Kendell sipped her rum. "You make us sound like some paranormal detective agency."

"It's not for me to direct what you do with your skills, but the more help Myles can secure, the easier it will be for him to complete the chores we have for him."

Myles was trying not to become intoxicated, but dealing with a loa of the dead had a way of making him drink more than he ought to. He poured another glass. "That brings us back to why we requested this meeting. Once we do lay our hands on your cane, how difficult will it be getting it to you?"

The voodoo loa set his glass on the table, empty once again. "Distance only exists for the living. My connection to you is ever present. There is, however, a problem. That voodoo bitch Marie Laveau managed to lock my staff into the world of the living. You'll need to learn how to free it. Until you do, I won't be able to take possession."

Peachy. Myles was beginning to think every spirit he turned to for answers was just going to hand him another problem. "And how do we do that? If Madam de Galpion does have the walking stick, she's not going to let it go. If she doesn't, we'll need someone else to remove the spell— which, of course, we know nothing about. I thought you were supposed to help."

"My friend, if it were easy, I wouldn't need to rely on you."

Kendell returned her glass to the table. "Maybe if we knew a little more about how your cane was stolen, we might have a better idea of where to look. How did Marie Laveau learn about it?"

"I was betrayed by a fellow loa of the dead. The time will

come for me to take revenge, but for now, you need only worry about finding my cane."

Myles wondered how many pieces were in this magical jigsaw puzzle. "So someone from Guinee told Marie Laveau about your cane and, presumably, that you would be on the Mardi Gras float. She told Archibald Malveaux about it so he could steal it. Then he brought it back to her, and she locked it to this world. That was quite the compensation for a curse that didn't even effect Archibald himself."

"The cane was never meant for Malveaux," said Baron Samedi. "He was only to be the thief. Madam Laveau cast the Malveaux curse *after* the cane was stolen. The lust for power that runs through that family is nothing more than a burglar's desire for wealth. But Marie was not to be trifled with. There are aspects of the curse you have yet to discover."

7

Kendell had never minded her job at the coffee shop on Frenchmen Street. The small café was lined with books and frequented by locals from the Bywater and Marigny. Being a barista there felt more like welcoming friends into her home than actual work.

She finished straightening up a shelf of cozy mysteries. "I'm headed out."

"See you tomorrow." The day manager had covered for Kendell so many times she was more like a caring sister than a boss.

Despite the heat and humidity of summer, she closed her eyes and raised her face to enjoy the warmth of the sun.

The sound of a car slamming to a stop in front of her brought her back to the realities of her mission. The M highlighted with skulls in gold leaf on the back door of the black Lincoln limousine made it all too clear who was inside. Kendell was ready for battle even before the door opened.

As she expected, Colin Malveaux sat in regaled luxury in the back seat. "Get in."

"You must be daft."

He turned toward her. "If I meant you harm, I wouldn't have bothered coming myself. We need to talk."

She took a quick look back at the coffee shop. The manager nodded at her as if to say *I'll contact Myles.* Kendell returned the nod before entering the car, hoping Malveaux wouldn't do anything foolish.

The man who'd combined the two beings that had caused so much suffering sat opposite her. He spread out his hands so she could have a thorough look at her adversary. "What do you think of my attire?"

His long black coat draped the back seat, revealing an inner lining of red silk with embroidered purple fleurs-de-lis. A vampire would have found something less conspicuous. "You look like an idiot. If you were wearing a business suit like a normal professional, I could at least respect your sense of taste."

He simply shrugged. "The best of anything is often an acquired taste. Even so, I'm sure you noticed something is missing."

"I don't have your fucking cane." She hadn't meant to swear, but he really brought out the vulgarity in her.

"I know you don't. I have my people watching your people. But really? You think a handful of ragtag musicians can outmatch my wealth when it comes to searching the Quarter? But that's not what I wanted to talk about. You must realize every memory your boyfriend has of his abduction is also in my brain. I too know who kidnapped me, who was on that raft of a boat, and who was present at the exorcism bonfire."

Divulging what he knew was uncharacteristic of him. She wondered if that was a strategic play by Lincoln Laroque or the careless arrogance of Baron Malveaux.

"Why tell me?"

"Because I want you to see me as a competitor, not an enemy. I was in Guinee for over a hundred and fifty years. I know the conflict that rages between the loas of the dead. That fool of a boyfriend of yours has chosen a side. But he's not the only one with a baron backing him up. And mine still rules over one of the gates to the *deep waters.*"

She knew she was being threatened but couldn't identify the specifics of the peril. "I think you'll find it's more than just Baron Samedi who wants his cane returned."

"You don't get it. Everyone dies—me, you, your boyfriend, your bandmates, everyone. And whether that's today or decades from now, everyone passes through the gates of Guinee. Should I win this competition and secure the cane, you'll want me as a friend, not a foe. You've seen what happens to those trapped in my realm."

She realized the man's avarice wasn't contained to the living. "And if I help you—assuming you do find the cane first—you'll see to it that everyone I care about makes it safely to the *deep waters* when it's their time?"

The man's smile was nauseating. "I only wanted you to be clear on what cards I'm holding. The stakes are higher than you realize."

~

THE SMELL of Baron Malveaux's pipe tobacco still permeated the leather sofa and desk chairs in the bank's once-hidden office. Until the Laurette mansion's remodel was complete, the office was where he felt most at home. The idea that he would soon occupy his arrogant son's ultimate achievement gave him a feeling of warmth that eluded most business transactions.

By throwing enough money at contractors, he'd been assured even the mammoth wreck of a house could be rebuilt in something approaching a reasonable timeframe. The hidden diaries that had driven him to purchase the dump no longer interested him. He'd gained far more than control over the baron, but gaining the perspective of his ancestor had only left him empty. Ultimate power in life paled compared to being a loa of the dead.

He passed his secretary as he left the office. "I'll be out for the day."

Not that his whereabouts mattered, but he liked the idea that his employees would sigh with relief at being free of him for the afternoon. That made their fear at his return all the more satisfying.

Neither side of his personality enjoyed walking the handful of blocks from the opulent bank to Delphine's rundown shack, but he needed to confront her in person and on her own turf. She needed to know at a gut level that even hiding in her voodoo cave would be meaningless when faced with his ire.

He considered busting down the door, but due to its

rotting frame, the action might be taken as unintentional. He knocked on what appeared to be the most solid board of the siding, so weather-beaten the paint color couldn't be identified.

The door opened to a dark room and a tired Delphine.

"Did we have a meeting scheduled?" she asked.

He pushed her aside, not waiting for an invitation to enter. "You know why I'm here."

"I told your goons I don't have your damn walking stick."

She didn't appear to have a chair worthy of his noble derriere. In exasperation, he chose her gaudy throne and kicked his feet up onto her worktable. "Bullshit."

"Fine. I'm lying. Go ahead and ransack my shop and home looking for it. But you, above all people, know what will happen if you overturn the wrong jar."

He liked it when she was being testy. Irritating someone so thoroughly made him feel alive. "If you don't have it, you know who does." A feeling of cold hatred swept up from his bowels. "You gave it to that fucking swamp witch, didn't you? What was it? Payment for her services? I'll bring in a dredging team and turn that bayou into a golf course."

"It wouldn't do you any good. She passed to the *deep waters* not long after our meeting with her."

He balled his fists. *Finally, an adversary I can fuck with when I win.* "That stringy-haired granddaughter of hers. The one that pointed the shotgun at us. She's got it. Where do I find her?"

"You don't. It took me half my life before the old swamp witch invited me to her lair. I only know she's dead because of the change in the curse. There's a youthful, determined spirit that replaced the wisdom of age."

He dropped his feet from the table and glared at her. "Make contact with her. I want to make a deal."

"You really think it's that easy? The old witch told you there's a separation between her magic and my voodoo. I couldn't even enter her house. What makes you think her granddaughter will want anything to do with me? If you want to find her, you'll have to do it yourself."

Though he enjoyed the prospects of that new challenge, Delphine had wronged him, and as a powerful businessman, he couldn't ignore that. "You should have brought the cane to me. It's mine. I will hold you personally responsible until what's mine is returned."

"Now I'm saying bullshit. You stole that staff from Baron Samedi. It rightfully still belongs to him, but until he steps forward to claim it, I'll do everything in my power to make sure you don't regain control over the gate to the afterlife."

He got up and straightened his jacket. "I know about your work with that sexy, witchy guitarist. I'm just begging for any excuse to bring her down to the gutter of my depravity, but I thought I'd give you a chance to do the right thing first. Since you can't help me, perhaps with the right incentive, I can get her or her fool of a boyfriend to intensify their search."

"Leave Kendell and Myles alone. This isn't their fight."

He gave her an appraising stare. "So you'll help me?"

"I can't help you find the new swamp witch, but if you can make contact, I'll do what I can to facilitate the negotiation. You've already done enough harm to people."

~

DELPHINE HAD ALWAYS BEEN a thorn in his paw, but she still had her uses. Colin knew her offer of help was all about maintaining a modicum of control over how the cane was used, but he would deal with that challenge when he came to it. The first priority was to find the damn thing. At least he had a concrete lead, even if he didn't know the girl's name, where she lived, or really anything about her other than the fact that she knew how to handle a shotgun. He realized that criterion didn't narrow the field of Southern women very much.

He pulled his Ford Expedition into the familiar gravel parking area. Unlike his last visits, a gleaming aluminum airboat sporting a powerful V8 engine was moored to the battered dock.

The boat's pilot rushed up to greet him. "We're all set to go, Mr. Malveaux. I've plotted the most likely location of your island on my GPS. We should be there in less than half an hour."

"That's just the start of our search. Did you pack the overnight gear?"

The stocky man had a tan so deep Colin wondered if it was ethnicity or sunbaked. "I've got provisions for three days."

"That young woman will have lived much of her life in the bayou. I find it hard to believe she'd have traveled far after her grandmother's death."

The pilot fired up the massive engine, which effortlessly spun the six-foot propeller. "People out here either live their whole lives in the bayou or escape as soon as possible for the city. Either way, we'll find your answer before our adventure ends."

Instead of heading toward the river, the pilot swung the shallow draft boat directly toward a mat of water hyacinth and gave the engine all the throttle it could handle. For a moment, Colin thought *pilot* was all too accurate a title as the man at the controls glided the craft over the foliage as if about to take flight.

Looking back, Colin saw a wide swath of open water where the airboat had cut its path through the foliage. If the witch was still on the island, she'd have plenty of warning of his approach, though, as with her grandmother, the woman probably didn't need the notification.

The trip that had taken half a day by pole boat passed in less than an hour by airboat. "Does that island up ahead look like what you remember? If not, there are two or three other possibilities we can check out before dusk."

The dark cypress grove on the opposite side of the scrub forest was enough of a reminder for Colin. "That looks like the place. Swing around as close as you can to the trees, and I'll walk the rest of the way along the shoreline. Shouldn't take me long to find out what I want to know. If this is the place, I'll be spending the night here. You can camp in the boat."

The airboat swung a sharp ninety-degree turn toward the island. Though the engine had been shut down, Colin's ears still rang from the racket. The craft came to a gentle bump against the grassy shore.

"Sure you don't want to take a gun with you?" the pilot

asked. "People and gators out here aren't too accepting of strangers."

"I'll be fine. If the person I'm looking for is out here, a gun won't do me much good, and a gator wouldn't dare bite me."

Though the walk across the marshy ground was less dramatic than cutting through the disorienting forest, making the trek alone added a little hustle to Colin's steps. As he rounded a jetty, he lost sight of the airboat. Turning to look into the tall trees draped with Spanish moss, he saw the dilapidated cabin exactly where he remembered.

He could tell even before he approached the ladder that the house was deserted, as if the witch had been holding everything together through force of will. With her gone, the whole compound was deteriorating to dust.

He hadn't expected to find her alive. Delphine might not always know what she was doing, but even she wouldn't have misread the death of a powerful witch. Carefully, he ascended the ladder, hoping the boards would hold for one last visit.

The slashed screen door hung limp on its hinges. The old hag wasn't slumped over dead in her chair, which came as a relief.

He stood in the middle of what at one time must have been a living room meant for children and entertaining but was now nothing but desolation. "What am I doing here? Clearly, your granddaughter took any writings you might have left behind." The part of him that maintained the old baron's memories insisted he was missing something important.

The place barely had the basics to support life. He tried the kitchen faucet and was rewarded with brown goop oozing from the tap. Looking out the window and higher into the tree, he spotted a water tank lodged in the upper limbs. A pump had to be somewhere, but with the witch gone, the pipes were quickly filling with rust and sediment. He flipped a switch next to the sink. The bare bulb hanging from the ceiling attempted to radiate light but quickly faded back to darkness. *Must be battery powered.*

Sunset turned the ancient tree trunks from forbidding sentinels to welcome guardians as the light crept below the dense foliage above. Though old and withered, the woman must have found peace in the hardship of living on the island. He stared out across the bayou. Deep in the swamp, a flicker of light indicated someone was camping on a neighboring island.

8

*K*endell found it hard to believe Madam Delphine de Galpion was standing in her doorway. Though she and the voodoo priestess had become something resembling friends, that was before the woman stole Baron Samedi's cane.

"Come in," Kendell said. "This must be important, for you to come to me."

Delphine almost never left her shop, especially not in early afternoon. She looked tired. "It is. I've tried to shield you from further involvement in the Malveaux curse, but I'm afraid events have progressed beyond my control."

Cheesecake gave the dark woman a low-pitched growl before relinquishing the chair by the window.

Myles wasn't much more welcoming. "We're aware of Colin Malveaux, the people he used to be, and his search for Baron Samedi's walking stick. Do you still have it?"

"Direct as always. I did have it, but I don't any longer.

Colin Malveaux is headed out to the bayou to confront the witch who's guarding it. He won't find her, but with him out of the city, I no longer can keep tabs on what he's up to."

Kendell paced in front of the sunlit windows as Cheesecake walked with her. "So you did steal it. That would explain why the girls have come up empty searching the shops and why Professor Yates hasn't had any better luck. It would have been nice if you'd told us sooner. You could have saved us a lot of unnecessary work."

"By *not* telling you, I hoped you wouldn't run afoul of Colin. He's not to be trusted. And just in case anyone else is looking for the cane, it wouldn't be the worst idea to keep up the search as a distraction."

Myles leaned back in the couch with that smug look that made Kendell crazy. "Let me guess, you want our help but aren't willing to tell us anything. Your secrecy didn't work out so well for me last time."

"I'm not going to apologize for keeping Marie's secrets. But you're right in that I need your help. I'll tell you what I can. Together, we can still stop Colin."

Kendell was discomfited by his antagonism of Delphine. "What do you need us to do?"

"You and I spent a considerable amount of time modifying the curse. It's time we put that spell to work. In Colin's arrogance, he wears as many of the baron's old things as possible. You can access those objects to see where he is and what he's up to. More importantly, you can talk to Sanguine Delarosa, granddaughter of Agnes Delarosa. Sanguine is now the guardian of the curse. She's gone into hiding with the Samedi cane, but because you're now a part of the curse, you two can communicate."

Kendell hadn't forgotten her sessions in Delphine's voodoo library. They'd damn near killed her. That wasn't the kind of thing she'd forget, but since the spirits of the women Baron Malveaux had held hostage were freed, she had considered the job completed. "How is it I'm just now hearing about this mysterious witch? If she's associated with the curse, I would have expected to encounter her during our sessions." She sat on the ottoman. At her feet, Cheesecake kept a watchful eye on Delphine as if unsure if she was friend or foe.

"Think of the Wiccan witches as Marie's insurance policy," Delphine said. "For generations, those who followed her weren't half as skilled as you are now. The spirit women in Guinee had a lot to do with holding Baron Malveaux in the afterlife, but they weren't alone. Only the highest voodoo priestess was told of the swamp witches' roles in protecting Marie's spells. Agnes and I were silent associates. We knew of each other, and that was enough, but you and Sanguine are locked together." She interlaced the fingers of her hands. "You two are like two halves of a cage."

"So if I can keep track of Colin Malveaux's movements and talk to Sanguine, I can keep her one step ahead. How do I do it?"

"The glasses you found in Fleurentine Laurette's possessions weren't from her husband the baron, but I assume you already figured that out. They were a specialty of Marie Laveau's. Someday, I'll tell you the story of the glassblower that created them, but for now, know you can use them to communicate with Sanguine. Get comfortable in a quiet, dark room, and put them on. As she's the one guarding the curse, she'll be able to instruct you on how to access the objects being worn by Colin."

Myles leaned forward on the couch. "Wait. If Kendell can contact Sanguine and she has the cane, why don't we just hook her up with Baron Samedi? You can break whatever spell Marie put on the staff holding it to the living. He can get his walking stick back, and this whole thing will be over."

Kendell remembered learning Occam's razor in a philosophy class. *The simplest answer is often the correct one.* "Is there any reason Baron Samedi couldn't manifest next to her? It does seem like the most logical solution."

Delphine shook her head. "Marie thought of that possibility long ago. That headpiece Pierre Boudreaux fabricated wasn't just from an ordinary lump of silver. She secured sixteen pieces of eight from the pirate Jean Lafitte. Those coins carried the symbol of the Catholic church. Blessed silver can't be taken to the nether world. A spell does hold the headpiece to the staff, but it's not in any of Marie's writings—not even in the journals Lincoln Laroque gave me as payment for the voodoo fetish containing the baron's spirit. I can't break a spell without first knowing how it was cast."

Kendell wondered how many of Marie's writings were scattered throughout the city. "If you don't have the diary and the Laroque family didn't have it, where else could it be?"

"Baron Archibald Malveaux didn't get along with his

son, but he doted on his granddaughter. The journals the family owned came from the baron through his granddaughter. His son, however, liked to keep things hidden—even from his own daughter."

Kendell remembered all too well how Samantha Laurette had found the cursed pipe tool in the Laurette mansion. "So we're back to digging in the walls of the buildings Anthony Laurette designed?"

"He would have kept close something as valuable as the key to unlocking the Samedi cane."

The mansion had been in a pretty bad state the last time she and Myles talked with Samantha.

"The previous owner was trying to unload the place. Any idea who owns it now?"

"I'll give you one guess, but you won't need it."

Kendell swore under her breath. "So Colin Malveaux is the only one who might possess information on how to separate the two pieces—the person who would be least likely to allow that to happen."

"Nothing is ever straightforward. Without that diary, I don't know what exactly happens when the headpiece is removed. Colin bought the old Laurette mansion and is having it remodeled. I have to believe what he's really doing is searching for the journals Marie left to the baron's son. If there's a way to bring down Colin Malveaux, it'll be in those writings. They'll be in code. Keep those glasses safe. They could be our only way of deciphering her hundred-year-old secret plan."

Myles got up, paced like someone on a mission, and ticked off items on his fingers. "Right. Contact the witch over the curse network. Use the old cursed items to keep an eye on Colin Malveaux. Retrieve Marie Laveau's diary from the walls of the Laurette mansion while it's being remodeled by Colin's contractor. Figure out what it says. Bring the cane and diary to you for separation. Then contact Baron Samedi to come get his stick. Oh, and I'd better not forget we need to maintain our cover story of searching New Orleans's shops and homeless to keep Joe Cazenave and his boss Luther Noire from getting any ideas of what we're really up to. If they get their hands on the walking stick, who knows where it'll end up. Anything I'm missing?"

Kendell nudged him as he passed her. "You could lose the attitude."

"I'd just like to know what she's going to be doing while we're risking our necks… again."

"After you bring me the cane and curse diary, I'll have my work cut out for me. Undoing something Marie Laveau bound together is no simple matter."

❧

ONCE DELPHINE HAD LEFT, Myles and Cheesecake settled into their usual spots on the couch. Kendell turned the glasses with their green-tinted lenses in her hand. "I suppose we should start with the simplest task. Contacting Sanguine, at least, doesn't carry the risk of getting caught by one of Colin's people."

"There's nothing simple regarding what you're about to do. You've got every reason to be hesitant. Accessing that curse in Madam de Galpion's shop left you convulsing during the session and drained afterward."

That had also left her with remnants of Baron Malveaux's soul, which she'd unintentionally transferred to Myles during their sexual encounters.

"If you notice a change in me, you have to say something," she said. "I promise I'll take it seriously."

He reached over to the ottoman and held her hands. "I didn't know what I was seeing last time. We know better what to look for now. Would you feel more comfortable if Cheesecake went along with you?"

Kendell looked at the teddy bear of a dog lounging in the sun. "She looks so harmless in this reality but a total protector wolf in the other. I don't want to intimidate Sanguine—not on this first meeting."

"Fair enough. We'll be right here if you need us."

She couldn't imagine his proposal was anything other than for moral support, but she'd learned not to discount any offer of assistance. "I just wish I had a walk-in closet or something. Conducting this meeting in the bathroom doesn't seem very respectful. But it's the only totally dark room in the apartment."

He kissed her on the forehead. "I'm sure she'll understand."

Kendell grabbed a pillow off the couch and headed to the small bathroom. Sitting in the claw-foot tub would at least beat conducting the chat on the toilet. With the door closed and the lights off, she confronted one of her lingering fears, that of small, dark places. Being in a city with constant entertainment, her apartment was never truly dark or quiet. She liked it that way.

I'm not really alone. The thought helped her combat her anxiety. Sitting on the pillow in the old enameled cast-iron tub, she fumbled with the glasses until they sat comfortably on her face. "Sanguine Delarosa, if you're out there, I need to talk to you." She repeated the request several times, hoping for an answer but at the same time feeling a little silly.

The lenses of the glasses glowed, but from her peripheral vision, she knew the room remained dark. A woman in her early twenties, younger than Kendell, bent her neck back and shook her hair out of her face. "I've been expecting you. That asshole's invaded my island and is after me. I hope you've got a plan."

"Then you know of the work Delphine de Galpion and I did on the curse. I need access to the items Colin Malveaux has on him. If I can track him, I can keep you one step ahead until we can find a way to return the cane to Baron Samedi."

The young woman crossed her arms and glared at Kendell through the glasses. "Then what? We're not going to have many shots at this guy. Just because you deny him his little stick, that doesn't make him harmless. Far from it. I don't mind playing the bait while you catch this fucker, but catch and release is for schmucks. This is the best shot we're likely to get at this guy. *He's* after *us*. That's an advantage."

Kendell suppressed her sigh of disappointment. Apparently, everyone had their own agenda. "What do you have in mind?"

"Kill him."

She stared disbelievingly at the woman in the glasses. "That doesn't seem a little extreme to you?"

"You don't try to rehabilitate a nutria. Vermin need to be dealt with decisively. We have something he wants. That puts us in the driver's seat. Use the power you have while you can. I'll give you access to his little trinkets, but you'd better come up with something better than just keeping an eye on him. I'm not letting you know where I am until you've got a better plan."

Kendell really wanted to like the girl, but the last thing she needed was one more person who thought they knew what to do better than she. "Fine. Just tell me how to access the curse. I can at least keep you safe from his plan."

"Get something that belonged to Baron Malveaux, something that is still under the curse. Then find a map of the area and put on those glasses. That's about it. You'll feel the baron's object gravitate toward a spot on the map like a compass needle. With the glasses on, you'll get a better look at his exact location. As for listening in on who he's talking to and what he's doing, well, you're not ready for that yet."

Kendell wondered if that was what it would have been like to have a sister. "I've spent my time in the dark energy of the curse. My boyfriend has taken me to Guinee. It's not like I'm unfamiliar with what happens."

"Fine, but don't come crying to me when he takes possession of your soul. You open that kind of link, and there's no telling who's really in control." She smirked like a know-it-all. "That's the problem with voodoo. Y'all think you can gain control over others by accessing the afterlife.

Wicca is more about existing in the here and now, about living as one with nature."

Kendell really wasn't in the mood for a lecture. "So how do I listen in on his conversations?"

"Take the cursed object and do what you're doing now with me, but hold the item and try to imagine what he looks like. And keep your mind quiet. If you can hear him, he can hear you. These connections are never only one-way. The deeper you get into his mind, the more you open your own."

The thought of once again opening her soul to the baron made her grip the rough lip of the tub so hard it threatened to cut her fingers. "Now I understand your warning. I'll only keep an eye on him, but at least there's another trick in my arsenal if I need it. I'll be back in contact once I know something."

"That's not going to work for me. I can't just find a lovely spot to chat while I'm navigating the bayous. You can reach me either in the morning just before dawn or dusk after the sun sets. Think up a plan soon. There's a storm coming. The animals have already started going to ground. I don't want to be caught out here with nothing more than a magic stick when Mother Nature lets loose her fury."

～

MYLES NEARLY FELL ASLEEP WAITING for Kendell to get done with her bathroom conversation. He sat up straight, however, when he heard the door open. She looked more pissed than anything else.

"How did it go?" he asked.

She described their latest challenging partner and relayed what she'd said. "I suppose if I was the one on the run, I too would want something more definitive than handing off my pursuer's cane to someone else."

Though the suggestion of murdering someone so powerful shouldn't have even been a consideration, Myles had to admit the idea had its merits. "We have seen the baron's old possessions used to kill others, and even to me, the deaths looked like accidents."

"I'm not killing anybody. Only I have control of the cursed objects, so you're talking about me doing the deed, and I'm not doing it. End of story."

He nodded. "It might not even work, anyway. The curse was aimed at the baron's offspring, not the man himself. Even though part of Colin is made up of Lincoln Laroque, the man never seemed very worried about the items even after you'd modified the curse. I wouldn't be surprised to find Delphine gave him a charm or something for his safety."

She resisted the urge to get into another fight about Delphine and her motives. "So you agree killing him is out."

"Returning him to Guinee wouldn't solve anything. Baron Samedi said he was betrayed by someone in the afterlife. That person used Archibald Malveaux and Marie Laveau. Sending Colin to Guinee might only return the servant to the master. I was just saying Sanguine had a point, not that it was a good idea. But even if everything works perfectly and we get the cane back to Baron Samedi, what's to stop Colin from trying something else? I wouldn't put anything past him. We need to look beyond the next move and see this as a much larger game."

Kendell didn't need reminding that Myles had suffered a fate worse than death when the baron was in charge of his body. No other living person would understand better than Myles the depths the baron would sink to.

She sat next to him. "We have to stop him. I get that. I also understand Sanguine's viewpoint that we have the upper hand, and that's not a situation destined to last once we're rid of the cane. What do you think we should do?"

"I wish I had an answer. It feels like we're constantly reacting to something. Maybe if we can get our hands on that diary, we might finally understand our position better. There has to be more in it than how to take a headpiece off a cane. If all this drama in life is just a game being played out among the loas of the dead, we need to ensure Baron Samedi regains his full power. Getting the cane back to him has to be our first priority."

Of all the activities Myles had listed, breaking into the Laurette mansion while it was being dismantled and rebuilt sounded the most foolhardy. Even if they didn't get caught, poking around a building in even worse shape than it had been when Samantha Laurette owned it sounded like a good way to end up in the hospital.

"We're going to need to get that journal before it lands in Colin's office," she said, "but the mansion must be crawling with workers."

"I worked construction for a summer in college. That's how I met Charlie. If anyone can get me on a demolition crew, he can."

She wasn't sure working around a bunch of burly thugs with sledgehammers and crowbars was any safer than sneaking in on their own. "What good will that do? They must be watching everything that gets taken out of there. If he weren't out chasing after Sanguine for the cane, I bet Colin would be overseeing the operation. In his absence, he wouldn't leave the excavation in the hands of someone he didn't completely trust. Remember, Baron Malveaux was wandering around in your body. I'd imagine a lot of people might recognize your face."

"He's after the cane. He may not even know about the diary. And as for my appearance, I won't be wearing expensive, outdated attire. He was pretty disgusted by my normal streetwear. First thing he did was get a new suit. Then he spent all his time with the high and mighty. No one in the trades is going to recognize me as a day laborer. As a member of the demolition crew, I'll be able to find out if they've already found the diaries or anything else of interest."

She didn't like the idea of Myles being so close to Colin's people. "But even if you are working and run across the journals, there's no way you could sneak them out."

"Not during the day, but as a worker, I can fix it so we can slip in at night when no one's watching. Charlie will probably have an idea or two. When it comes to being sneaky, he's my go-to guy."

She could see how that could work. "Just be careful. Calling in the cavalry to rescue you again isn't going to help keep our activities inconspicuous."

9

Myles tugged at the legs of his tight jeans. Bits of paint and drywall mud that wouldn't come out in the wash crumbled in his fingers. His worn steel-tipped boots were cramming his toes together. Only the T-shirt felt halfway decent, but by the end of the day, it would be destined for the trash.

"You don't have to do this," he said.

Standing next to him as they looked over the three stories of rotting wood, plaster, and history, Charlie sounded more enthusiastic. "Are you kidding? I've been begging to go on another treasure hunt with you since the day you found that WWII airplane."

"I'm not expecting anything that cool today. Even if we do find something, we won't be taking it to the newspapers." Myles knew that the real reason Charlie reminisced rhapsodically to any woman who'd listen to his tales of daring adventure was simply to get her into his bed.

Hanging around with Myles provided the Lothario with plenty of romantic ammunition.

"Doesn't matter. Mystery, intrigue, ghosts, danger—you couldn't keep me away if you tried. What's your plan if we do find something?"

Myles knew the mansion well enough from his talks with Samantha while she was trying to clean up the property she'd inherited from her family. "There's a dumbwaiter at the back of the house. It was installed for one of the old people who'd probably lived their whole life in the place. Anyway, it got wallpapered over decades ago. Up in the attic is a hidden crawl space that houses the pulleys. If we find anything, we can stash it in there. You wouldn't happen to have an in with the night watchman would you?"

Charlie smiled at him in the mischievous way he reserved for an upcoming conquest. "You mean night watch*woman*?"

"Even better. Tonight after everyone leaves, I'll leave it to you to find a suitable distraction for her while I slip in to retrieve our booty."

The rogue adjusted his overalls over his bare chest. "We'd better get to work. Once the humidity hits in full force, we'll be sweating through the thickest denim."

Though Myles dreaded the feeling of his jeans becoming more a second skin than protective covering, he knew Charlie would be looking forward to taking breaks outside while the neighborhood women ogled the glistening, muscular workman.

The foreman motioned for them to join him. "Most of

my skilled workers are removing the walls in the upstairs bedrooms. We're trying to salvage and restore as much of the original architecture as possible. I'm putting you two to work in the attic. Not much damage you can do up there. I need that space back to the studs by the end of the day. Don't get hurt, don't get lazy, don't get sticky fingers, and we'll get along fine."

Myles remembered the drill. College guys were constantly looking to pick up some quick cash. What few of them realized was construction was a brutal occupation. Not many of the uninitiated lasted more than a day, so foremen seldom handed out assignments they didn't think could be completed by the end of the shift.

The old mansion looked much worse than Myles remembered, which wasn't a surprise. Ripping away the old wallpaper revealed only what old-fashioned décor the past generation wanted hidden. At least with the rugs gone, the rodent smell had diminished. However, the stench of rotting wood wasn't a huge improvement. He let Charlie lead the way even though he'd been there enough to know the layout.

The overheard conversations on the third floor weren't in English. Immigrant labor wasn't only cheaper, it was more reliable.

"Jesus, they expect us to haul equipment up that rickety ladder?" Charlie was always braver outside, where women might overhear, than deep in the job site.

A stocky kid who looked to be the foreman's son handed them a couple of pry bars. "For now, this is all you'll need. Start with the upper wallboards and work your way down.

That way, if there's any surprises, they run away rather than jump out at you."

Myles recalled his summer spent pulling down hurricane-damaged houses. After years of being vacant, at least of human life, the run-down shacks were teeming with unwanted bugs and rodents.

"Any guesses on what they used for insulation?" he asked.

"It sure as hell ain't fiberglass batting. I can tell you that." The kid turned and yelled something in Spanish to the workers, who jumped to, as if he himself was the owner.

Carrying the heavy steel bar up the extendable ladder felt pretty iffy as it shifted from side to side. Once upstairs, without the noise of workmen and conversations, Myles tried to access any secretive human energy that might inhabit some long-lost artifact.

"Any thoughts on where we should start?" Charlie swung his pry bar like a baseball bat.

Myles knew he was really asking if he'd detected any treasure. "Start at the front and work our way back, I suppose. I'll take this wall. You take that one."

In the dust-speckled light filtering through the dirt-encrusted window, Charlie in his overalls could have passed for someone from another era. "Maybe if you took a load off, you might get a better feel for the room."

Reading energy did require as calm a place as possible. "Lying down on the job when we've just started work doesn't seem like the best way to keep this gig for the whole day. We're going to have to do this the hard way, my friend."

The boards came loose without a lot of undue force. The

bigger problem was staying clear of anything the old timbers were keeping secluded between the rafters. As though he was trying to make out a single voice in a room full of conversations, Myles knew items were there to be found but had no way of knowing where.

"Wow, damn." Charlie jumped back from the wall he was dismantling.

"Find something?"

He stepped aside to show an avalanche of cigarette butts that had recently occupied the wall. "And that's just the third board down. There must be an emphysema-load of cigs in this wall. I think we just discovered how great-grandpa got sick after he'd sworn off smoking."

"Pull off the bottom board next. That'll give the butts somewhere to drain while you work from the top."

That wasn't the first secret smoking spot Myles had run into. How the old folks managed to not burn down their houses by stashing their butts in the walls was a mystery.

"Any luck on your side?"

Myles had resorted to knocking on the boards before yanking them off the wall. "Well, once I get these guys trained up a bit, I should have enough cockroaches to rule the world. Other than that, just enough dust and mold to give me asthma."

"Hang on, I think I've got something." The way Charlie reached his arm down into the wall made Myles very uncomfortable.

"Remember what the foreman said. Don't go getting yourself hurt."

"Yes, *Mom*." Charlie reached down farther until his

whole arm was inside the wall. "Got it. As the cigarette butts were draining out, I saw it slipping toward a gap in the outer wall siding. Didn't want to lose it. Come here, and give me a hand. If you pry off the second board from the bottom, I think I can hand it to you."

On his way across the attic, Myles discretely closed the hatch to the ladder. The last thing they needed was someone checking on them just as they were discovering their treasure.

"What do you think it is?" he asked.

"Why don't you move your ass and open this wall so we can both find out? I hope I'm only imagining that something is tugging on the other side."

"Right."

The board crumbled as Myles put his weight behind the pry bar. Even when the board was clear, the space behind it was filled with the rotting remains of the half-destroyed wood. He bent down and started shoveling the debris away with his hands. At first, the wiggling dust made him want to reach for a hammer.

"That's me, by the way—just in case you were getting any ideas about decapitating one of my fingers."

Myles felt around until he found the wax-paper-covered book in Charlie's grasp. "This might be what we're looking for."

"You, maybe. I've still got my heart set on a trunk of Confederate bullion. Hell, I'd settle for a single bar stashed in this lovely wall."

Myles didn't wait for Charlie to get his arm out of the amalgamation of splinters that passed for boards. Pulling open the wax paper, he found layers of cotton and leather protecting the contents. "Whatever it is, someone went to a lot of work to make sure my army of cockroaches didn't eat it."

Charlie sat next to Myles on the bare wooden floor. "What does it say? Is it the journal you were looking for? If that's all you wanted, I could just stash it down my overalls. No foreman's going to go poking around down there after a hard day of work."

"You really think Kendell is going to touch it once it's been down your sweaty crotch? It's not worth the risk. Plus, we still have that gold to find for you."

By the end of the day, Myles remembered why he'd turned from construction to bartending. The party juice he had to clean off the counter and floor every night didn't compare to generations of bug and rodent turds.

～

KENDELL LOOKED in her black backpack, a match to the one Myles had slung over his shoulder. "How much stuff are we stealing? I thought we were just after the diary."

Without electricity to the mansion, the whole property was cast in shadows from the streetlights.

Myles in his black pants, shirt, and makeup looked every bit the stereotypical cat burglar. "Charlie stumbled across a couple of items he claimed as payment for his services. There's nothing that would cross the line out of petty larceny."

She hunched down in the bushes and peered at a woman

in a security-guard uniform sitting on the porch. Since she had only a gas lantern for light, reading her romance novel must have been hell on her eyes. Charlie nonchalantly strolled up the walkway. Immediately, the woman put down the book, but instead of a stern rebuke for the interloper, she smiled welcomingly.

"How does he do it?" Kendell asked.

Myles shook his head. "I've been trying to figure that out for years. In all the time I've known him, I haven't seen a single woman resist him for more than thirty seconds."

Kendell pouted at Myles. "You sound envious."

He smacked her on the butt. "I'm happier than he'll ever be, but that contentment has been paid for with years of frustration and disappointment. We'd better get moving."

With the guard sufficiently distracted by Charlie's attention, sneaking into the backyard of the dark mansion was almost disappointingly easy. The heavy chains and padlocks on the doors, however, made Kendell reconsider her momentary complacency.

"How the hell are we going to get inside without alerting the whole neighborhood?" She turned to Myles, expecting an answer.

He was nearly out of sight, though, as he rounded a wall that jutted out into the backyard. "Stay low and keep quiet."

She couldn't quite make out what the small square projection, running up the side of the house, had been used for. At no more than three feet square, the interior would be too small to be a room or even a closet.

Myles yanked at a board in line with his head, which gave way without a sound. "We stashed everything in this dumbwaiter, but we didn't dare try to use the pulley, with everyone poking around. Hopefully, the damn thing still works."

She could barely make out two metal cables inside the opening. He gave a firm tug on the closer one. Nothing moved, but from the debris that cascaded down the three-story shaft, she figured the convenience hadn't been used for some time. He used two hands for the second attempt. A muffled thud vibrated the ground at her feet.

"Shit. That must have been the counterweight," Myles said. "Give me a hand. This thing must weigh a hundred pounds. I can't have it come crashing to the ground."

She rushed to his side and grabbed the cable below his hands. "I think I've got it."

"That's better. We're slowly going to let it down hand under hand. Follow my lead."

The tendons in his forearms rippled his skin as his arm ascended the shaft then quickly darted below his other arm. Being right up against his side, she couldn't help breathing in his manly aroma generated from his hard day's work. Being attracted to the tough, rugged working type wasn't like her, but that was Myles, after all. Being sexually turned on by her boyfriend wasn't really a bad thing, but she figured the timing might not be optimal.

Though she could feel the weight on the cord, she wondered if she was contributing anything of real value to the endeavor. "Please tell me you loaded everything from the second story."

"Sorry. We were working in the attic. We've got to lower

this thing the entire height of the house. Just stick with me. We can do it."

His confidence gave her courage if not strength. By the time the bottom wheels of the car appeared in the opening, her arms where burning from the exertion.

"That's the back of the box," she said. "We still can't get the stuff out." Frustration and unresolved sexual tension were making her wish she'd stayed at home with her faithful dog, anxiously waiting her hero's return.

"Don't fret. We loosened the plywood while we had it upstairs."

The heavy wooden box finally came to rest against some stop inside the shaft.

"I hope Charlie appreciates what we had to go through for his greed," she said. "He'd better be charming the pants off that security guard."

"I'm positive he's doing his best. When it comes to women, he seldom gives anything less than his all." Myles pushed on the thin plywood, and it folded in half with a snap like cheap cardboard.

"You're not afraid someone's going to notice the hole in the wall tomorrow?"

Gingerly, he pulled the back of the dumbwaiter out through the gap. "It's all wallpaper inside the house. They won't get around to demoing the downstairs rooms for at least another week. If the journal Charlie found is what we're looking for, I have no intention of showing up for another shift."

Kendell suspected whatever creepy stuff Myles had found

in the walls wasn't a story she wanted to hear. In spite of her dedication to female equality, she was happy to leave some jobs to guys who didn't care how they looked or smelled at the end of the day. "Let's just get this stuff and get out of here."

"Is that a lack of confidence in my stealth abilities or Charlie's stamina?"

She suppressed a giggle. "Well, his advances on the security guard didn't look like they'd result in a long-term relationship. I doubt he's even planning on a one-night stand. Is there a term for a liaison that lasts less than an hour?"

"It takes me that long just to get a woman's number, but he is more the wham-bam-thank-you-ma'am type of lover." Myles pulled out a small tin box. "Civil War glass negatives —don't drop it. Most of what Charlie stashed away related to the war. I suspect someone wanted to hide their past but not destroy it."

Kendell carefully set the box in the bottom of her bag. "Must have been Anthony Laurette. I wonder if these pictures would show his transformation from Antoine Malveaux into the alias he clung to for the rest of his life."

"Speculate later. Grab this sword. It weighs a ton." He looked like some magician pulling the long scabbard from the small box.

"Leave it to Charlie to grab the longest cavalry saber he could find. He couldn't be satisfied with a nice little bowie knife? How much shit does he expect you to steal?"

"I'm impressed you know the difference, but I don't think his desire was for length so much as value." Myles finally handed her the wax-paper-wrapped book. "Once we got the bottom of the walls open, it was a cornucopia of historical garbage. That sword was the only big item. I'll have the rest out before you know it."

∿

TO KENDELL, hanging out in Myles's apartment was a bit like sneaking away for an illicit rendezvous. Even if they weren't meeting for romantic purposes, the dark brick man cave felt like an exotic escape from her daily life. The bags of booty had been left on his sagging couch, but she'd retrieved the wax-paper-covered diary.

"We have to open it," she said. "Even if we do give it to Delphine to figure out, I still need to make sure this is the journal we're looking for."

"No argument here. I only had a moment to peek at it in the attic. If it's not the right book, I can still show up to work on the construction crew tomorrow."

Kendell rubbed her fingers together before carefully peeling open their prize. Fine cotton, like an old-fashioned undergarment, was layered below the yellowed wax paper. A final sheet of thin, soft suede protected the fine-grained leather cover. "Someone went to a lot of work to protect it. Funny that they'd leave it in the walls with the bugs and mice, but it doesn't look damaged."

"I'll bet you were the kind of kid who tried saving Christmas wrapping paper. What does the damn book say?" He'd had the same impatience regarding her clothing on their first night together.

She handled the book the way she would a historic relic

from the New Orleans Historical Collection. "It hasn't been used much. The binding is still stiff. Whoever wrote in it didn't leave it lying around for anyone to read even before they secured it in the wall. Oh dear." She continued reading.

Soon, Myles lost his patience. "What. Does. It. Say?"

"The first page is not even encoded. Marie addressed it to 'the guardian of the Malveaux Curse'—that has to be Sanguine—and 'the inheritor.' Who do you suppose that is?"

Myles came around behind her to look over her shoulder at the book. "I can make a wild guess: you. As both the descendent of the baron Malveaux and Louis Broussard, you'd make the most sense as inheritor."

She knew that was going to be his answer though not being at the center of the problem would've been nice, for once. "It says the two of us have to work together under the instruction of a voodoo queen to go any further. The rest of the pages feel like they're glued together."

"So we can't even be certain this is the right book, but even if it is, we somehow need to get the cane, book, Baron Samedi, Sanguine, Madam de Galpion, and you all together at the same time and place."

Kendell put the book down and wrapped Myles in her arms. "It's a step forward. You did good. Sanguine has the cane, and I have the book. We just have to figure out how to get her here and make sure Delphine doesn't do something foolish like last time. I know you're not happy about it, but I'm going to have to trust her with the diary. She needs to get started figuring out how to open it. And finally, with you at my side, Baron Samedi won't be hard to call forth."

"Yeah, but Colin Malveaux is after Sanguine, we've got at

least one paramilitary team following your band, the dark web is full of discussions about finding Baron Samedi's cane, and what worries me most are the unknown dangers."

"Well, I wouldn't object if you called forth a host of the recently dead as a spirit army, but I'm not going to count on their support."

10

Colin was up before the morning light. Shadows cast by the predawn turned the cypress grove into an ominous region of ghosts and gators—exactly the type of place a swamp witch would go for safety. Invading another person's domain carried both the threat of being at a strategic disadvantage and the thrill of letting an adversary know no place was safe from him.

He packed up his overnight bag. The dead witch's lair had provided nothing useful, but as a base camp, it was one of the few places he would be at ease. From there on, he'd have to be on guard at all times. Looking at the bare, moth-eaten mattress, he regretted not having gotten a better night's sleep. Those were likely to be the last uninterrupted six hours he would experience for some time.

Descending the tree proved more hazardous than the climb. Each weathered board of the ladder snapped under his weight as if the dead witch was taking her last shot at killing him before he pursued her granddaughter. *I haven't forgotten your threat, old hag.* She must have known simply holding the leash wouldn't be enough for him. He was still baffled about why she'd tempted him with control of the curse if she could see the future, though.

He jumped the final six feet to the ground rather than suffering more splinters from the decaying wood. The noises from the swamp made him feel as though he was being watched as he worked his way along the shoreline back to the airboat. Cigarette smoke rose into the motionless air, letting Colin know he wasn't the only early riser.

"I hope you got a better sleep in that cabin than I did in the boat," the pilot said. "This bayou gives me the creeps. Something kept slamming into the hull, but every time I turned on the flashlight, it slunk away back into the marsh."

Small talk had never interested Colin, not as Lincoln Laroque and particularly not as Archibald Malveaux. "I'm headed into the cypress grove. My understanding is that your airboat can't go in there without damaging the hull, plus the noise would only alert the person I'm pursuing of my presence."

The pilot flicked the cigarette butt into the swamp. "I agreed to get you out here in my boat. There wasn't anything said about me traipsing through the swamp on foot. Me and my boat come as a set."

"I'm going alone. I could be a day, or I could be a week. Don't feel obligated to hang around. I'll call you when I'm ready to be picked up."

The man leaned against the bow of his boat and pointed

at the grove of trees. "There's no cell signal past this island. And that swamp can drain a battery as fast and unnoticed as a mosquito drinking blood."

"Fine. I'll expect you to fly your little boat out here each day at dusk. You know who I am, so you know the danger in crossing me. Continue making the trip until I turn up, even if it takes a year. Understood?"

"Yeah, I get it. So long as I get paid, you'll get no complaints from me. Any message you want me to deliver to your people back home?"

Colin couldn't imagine anyone he cared enough about to calm their fears, and no one could offer any useful help except Delphine. "Tell that voodoo priestess if I die out here, she's the first one I'm coming back to haunt."

Though he hadn't meant it as a joke, the pilot snickered before starting to unload the boat. "I wish I had some advice for you about surviving that swamp. You sure you don't want a gun? I've got both a rifle and a handgun. The gators out there can get pretty aggressive."

Even with that pack of provisions, Colin knew he'd have to live off the land at some point. "Leave me the rifle and ammunition. If I'm not here tomorrow when you come back, drop off another backpack of supplies. Hopefully, I can use this island as a base of operations."

"Will do, but I wouldn't count on returning here like you were commuting from home. That's a big swamp, and even those of us who live out here get lost sometimes. Take as much as you can with you. Mind telling me how you intend on getting around?"

The conversation was getting on Colin's nerves. "There's

an old rowboat at the base of the treehouse. I left a GPS transmitter in the cabin. My phone can pick up the signal even without cellular coverage. Wait a couple of hours before you head out. I don't want the noise waking up the whole bayou."

∿

COLIN LOADED the small boat with as many packs as he dared. Pushing off from the shore, he realized it wasn't as seaworthy as he'd hoped, but the leaks weren't gushing water. He sat on the center thwart and gave the oars a good hard pull against the water. Fortunately, they felt much more substantial than the hull.

He had only a rough idea of which direction light was coming from. As he watched the island recede behind the thick tree trunks, self-doubt crept in like the swamp water he continually had to bail out of the boat. As with his small plastic bucket, though, he had his need for the walking stick to keep him afloat and determined.

For the first few hours, his personal safety prevented him from wandering farther than eyeshot of the cabin high in the trees. *Stupid. Of course she's not this close to the island.*

As the sun rose over the tops of the trees, he threw away his foolish doubts and fears. He turned the boat away from the island and pulled at the oars with all his strength. If he was going to find the new swamp witch, he wouldn't do it by playing it safe.

By late afternoon, his arms were as useless as limp noodles. Between the physical exertion, heat, humidity, and bugs, he longed for a long soak in his spa, but thoughts of such luxuries only distracted him from his purpose. Ignoring the blisters on his hands. he grasped the oar handles and put his back into the effort.

The boat came to an abrupt stop, causing him to fall over backward into the water that had again seeped into the hull. Tired, blistered, bruised, and soaked, he climbed out of the boat to survey his latest discovery. He knew most men of lesser character would find his condition untenable, but the physical discomfort made him feel alive. The part of him that had spent so long in Guinee relished the pain like a prize fighter who'd just gotten serious about the contest. With a good hard pull from his legs, he beached the boat enough that it wouldn't float away.

He left the bags but grabbed a long-sleeve shirt. He threw it on and pulled it to his wrists. Without it, the chiggers living in the Spanish moss hanging from the tree limbs would see his bare arms as a buffet of human flesh, and he'd already suffered enough bug bites for one day. He pulled out the rifle and made sure it was loaded. The vegetation wasn't much different from that on the island he'd left that morning. He assumed snakes and alligators lurked in the tall grass at the water's edge. *No time like the present to utilize my survival training.*

Traversing the small landmass, which barely rose above the waterline, didn't take long. He'd nearly given up on looking for signs that any human had been there when he spotted a muddy rut in the reeds. From the sharp groove in the silt and the water lapping up the miniature canal, he guessed a small boat, though bigger than what he was using, had been beached there. The grass was still green, so the boat hadn't spent much time covering it. The mud held the crisp lines carved into it, so whoever had been there left not long before. With no other signs of human activity, he doubted a gator hunter had left the signs. Those guys weren't discrete about letting others know who'd claimed the spot.

He bent down to use the groove as a line of sight. Though he couldn't see the cabin in the trees he'd left that morning, from the position of the sun, he knew the boat's position hadn't lined up with where he'd started. As he stared through the trees, he held his breath. Off in the distance, he thought he saw a puff of smoke. Though it might have only been a trick of the late-afternoon light, he took on the steely-eyed determination he always felt when he sensed weakness in an adversary. He had a destination for the next day.

KENDELL SPREAD out the map of southeast Louisiana on her kitchen table and put on the green-tinted glasses. With the advent of GPS, she seldom studied such archaic forms of navigation, and even when she did, she used a computer so she could zoom in for a better look.

The letter opener she'd retrieved from Miss Fleur's trunk—secured in Minerva's garage—made her want to stab the location of Colin Malveaux on the map as though piercing his nonexistent heart.

"He's right here," she said. "Any idea of where that is, relative to the highway?"

Myles kept back from the table. "Maybe you should set that knife down first. Not that I don't trust you, but we've seen that curse in action enough times for me to be a little wary."

"Sorry. You're right. Even I have trouble not falling under the influence." *Of course, my being the primary aggressor of the curse might have something to do with my reaction.* She'd done her best to stay clear of the baron's remaining possessions, but to read Colin's whereabouts, she needed the damn monogrammed opener.

Myles set the ruler on the map then compared the distance to the key at the bottom. "He's ten-point-seven miles from the freeway. I think we can figure out his exact coordinates on the computer."

"It can't hurt. You figure out where he is, and I'll contact Sanguine. The sun must just be setting. I don't have much time."

He nodded toward the bathroom. "Go do your magic. I'll yell out the numbers once I have them."

Kendell hadn't adjusted to using the small private room for meetings, but she hadn't had time to come up with an alternative. "Are you out there? I have his location."

The glasses glowed eerily, indicating Sanguine was there. The face that came into view, however, made Kendell catch her breath. The woman hadn't been the height of fashion the last time they'd spoke, but the wild-eyed, dirt-stained face that greeted Kendell looked like something out of a horror movie. Her hair stuck to her face, tracing the rivulets of sweat that still flowed from her sunburned forehead. "Make it quick. If I need to double back tonight, I'll have to sleep in the boat. There aren't a lot of islands on this first leg of the chase."

Myles called out the numbers from outside the closed door.

"Did you get that?"

In spite of Sanguine's haggard appearance, she still managed a look of superior exasperation. "What good are numbers going to do me? Honestly. It's like you've got no idea how to use magic at all. Go get the map and put your *finger* on where he's camped out."

Kendell mumbled her irritation.

"And I know what you're saying, by the way. It's not like we're talking with our mouths and hearing with our ears. You're not wearing magical earplugs. Ever hear of telepathy?"

Despite the fact that Kendell was safe in her apartment while Sanguine was suffering out in the swamp, she couldn't ignore some irritations. "You could give me a break. I'm just trying to help."

"And I'm the one who's risking her neck. Trust me, you don't want to go down the road of who's responsible and who's shouldering the risk."

Even though Kendell knew Sanguine would hear her mentally, what she wanted to say was best done with words. "I'm sorry. You're right." She didn't try to hide her growing feelings of sisterly devotion. Some emotions didn't translate well into words.

"Don't worry about me. Colin still thinks he's the one

doing the pursuing. So long as I don't get too far in front of him and I keep making stupid moves like lighting a campfire, he should stay on my tail."

Kendell knew she had a long way to go with understanding the new form of communication, but the dominant impression she got from Sanguine was how easy it would be for a woman born to the swamp to lose the city slicker among the gators. In the realm of thought, Kendell had to admit the idea wasn't the worst to cross her mind, but giving in to the temptation of allowing a murder would remove the last barrier to becoming what she'd feared with Robert Johnson. *I am not a devil.*

"Then come up with a fucking better solution, sister."

"I'm working on it. But just so you know, if something unfortunate happens to Colin before we return the cane to Baron Samedi, we'll just be sending our adversary to a higher plane of existence."

"Fucking voodoo bullshit." Sanguine disappeared from the glasses before Kendell could respond to the telepathic insult.

---

11

*W*ith Colin searching the swamp, Kendell thought the team should meet to discuss strategy. The girls were looking tired from the exercise in deception.

"How are things on the streets?" she asked.

Joe was sitting unusually close to Scraper. "My guys had to swoop in and break up a fight after Scraper coldcocked a dude who'd been following her from store to store."

Kendell couldn't remember her bass-playing bandmate ever flirting with a guy—if that was even what she was doing.

"I didn't need the help," Scraper said.

Joe looked to be enjoying her attention. "Didn't say you did. That guy never saw it coming. But fights in the Quarter have a way of attracting other participants."

"I can usually tell when I'm being followed, but you were

on my ass before I had a chance to really express my feelings to that guy. You came out of nowhere."

Polly saved the group from further embarrassment. "It's getting to be slim pickings out there. During the last rainstorm, I couldn't even find a decent umbrella. Anything that even remotely resembles a walking stick is getting snatched up. Just to be safe, we'll start searching in teams of two. It'll slow us down, but the treasure seekers out there are getting a little handsy. It'll also double our shadowy protective guard."

Lynn drew lines through each street on the map they'd searched, with *X*'s corresponding to the shops just to ensure they hadn't missed anything. "You know, when I'm flirting with a guy, eventually I have to either let him get close or cut him loose. It's a game of cat and mouse where the mouse is toying with the cat. I'm worried the felines are growing tired of the pursuit."

The situation wasn't hard to imagine. The paramilitary force keeping an eye on the girls would be feeling like older brothers assigned to keep an eye on their little sisters as they went shopping. That was hardly the type of work the men were trained for, and if others were covertly keeping an eye on the women and their protectors, they weren't about to show themselves.

"We need to poke the dragon," Kendell said.

"What do you mean?" Myles asked.

"We're assuming Joe's guys aren't the only ones keeping an eye on the band. And if there's another group in the shadows, we have to accept they're watching the two of us as well. If we spend too much time with Delphine—or start wandering out to the swamp—they might catch on that the cane isn't still hiding in some unsearched back room."

Joe shifted uneasily on the couch. "Do you suspect Colin or Luther?"

Kendell hadn't wanted to express her reservations about the mysterious gentleman in the abandoned building. "When someone tells me not to trust anyone except those in the room, he goes to number one on my list of suspicious characters. You've done a lot for us. I do trust you. And you vouch for your team, who clearly would follow you to the gates of hell. But Luther's agenda doesn't mesh with ours. He's admitted to wanting the cane for himself, and that means he might have someone keeping an eye on the band's progress. As for Colin, even if he does know where the cane is, it would only make sense for him to keep tabs on us as well—just in case we stumble onto something."

Polly perked up. "If more men are watching us, maybe we can pit the groups against each other. Making men jealous is easy enough."

Kendell knew the allure of being pursued. "Easy, Helen of Troy, I don't want to start a war—just find out who's watching."

"There may be another way," Myles said. "If we acted like we'd found something, it might flush out our watchers."

Kendell inspected the map Professor Yates had pulled out with the circles indicating areas he'd searched with his equipment. "To fool Luther Noire, it'll have to be an actual enchanted object, and it'll have to be bigger than the trinkets we found from the baron Malveaux. Professor, could you increase the sensitivity of your equipment to pick up more than just the cane?"

Professor Yates loomed over Kendell's shoulder and looked down at the map. "I should be able to. I originally modified my lab equipment with the thought that an object from Guinee would put out so much energy it would be easily identified. If we're not trying to hide our activities, I can use more batteries to boost the sensitivity. My traveling snake-oil-salesman trailer is going to start giving me a workout to pedal around town."

Myles took the two maps, laid one on top of the other, and held them up to the window. "Start by searching the areas neither you nor the band have checked out yet." He set the maps down and turned to Kendell. "Once the professor finds something, we'll need to be stealthy at grabbing it. The more secrecy, the more likely our shadows will make themselves known."

"Leave that to me," Polly said. "With the four of us running around town, we've gotten pretty sneaky at losing our tails. We've got moves that would put a basketball team to shame."

∾

WITH THE RISK of unknown groups spying on everyone, Myles insisted all future meetings be held in more clandestine locations. If he were to see things from the pursuers' perspective, Kendell's apartment would be his first spot for setting up surveillance. Besides, between band practice and gigs, she was in constant contact with her bandmates. With Joe and his team constantly watching the girls, getting messages to him only involved Scraper giving him a flirtatious look. That left only the professor as the one out of the loop.

The con man's sideshow trailer had become something of a fixture around the Quarter. Taking the show on the road to the rest of the city, however, would've attracted more unwanted attention from the police than Myles felt was necessary. The Bywater became the logical solution. With its usual cast of bohemian artists, street performers, and musicians, the eclectic neighborhood welcomed the new addition as one of their own.

Myles had to watch his step on the uneven brick sidewalks. Between the brass bands practicing for their nightly street-corner gigs and the gutter punks sleeping off the previous night's adventures, finding someone to ask about the steam-punk fortune teller with the gypsy trailer proved a challenge. By noon, he'd walked the distance from Frenchmen Street to the Industrial Canal twice, each time being assured the crazy old man was just a couple of blocks away. He'd met an old gypsy woman whose trailer was little more than a shopping cart covered in colorful blankets, a young woman wearing scarves and little else, and a dirty, long-haired gentleman who couldn't speak in full sentences, but no Professor Yates.

"Hey, mister, are you looking for Professor Cornelius?"

Myles looked down at a young kid who'd stopped banging on his plastic five-gallon bucket. "You know him?"

"He used to pay me to find information about the marks

that were looking to have their fortunes told around Jackson Square."

Myles had suspected the professor had some kind of con going on. "Have you seen him recently?"

"He was dragging that heap of a trailer behind his bicycle toward the Ninth Ward yesterday. I kept thinking I'd see him heading home, but I never did."

Myles fished five dollars out of his jeans. "Thanks. If you see him, tell him Myles is looking for him."

The youth stashed the bill in his shoe. "You Myles?"

"Yep."

He tilted the bucket drum and pulled an envelope from underneath. "He said if anything funky happened and you came looking that I should give you this. Is he okay?"

Myles took a quick look inside and saw a map of New Orleans with red circles and newly marked X's. "I don't know, but if you hear something, there's another five in it for you. I'll be back this way before dark."

"And if you're not?"

Despite the heat, the hairs on the back of Myles's neck bristled. "Find Kendell Summer. Anyone from the homeless population should be able to direct you to her. Tell her what you told me, and give her the envelope. I'm writing *ten dollars* on the outside so there won't be any mistake on what she's to pay you. Understand?"

"You don't have to be a prick about it. Prof C is a friend of mine. I just hope he's okay."

"Me too."

Myles hustled the half block to a bike rental shop that specialized in self-guided tours. The black single-speed cruiser wasn't much to look at, but it would beat walking. He wasn't crazy about crossing the Industrial Canal bridge. Some areas of New Orleans he avoided out of personal safety and some out of respect for those living there. The lower Ninth Ward encompassed both criteria.

As soon as he got off the bone-jarring overpass, he checked behind himself to see if he'd been followed. The people of the Bywater weren't happy about authorities patrolling their neighborhood, so if someone had been keeping tabs on him through the morning, he'd have heard about it.

If he did have a tail, they were doing a damn fine job of being invisible. He started his grid search of the area by following the most redeveloped streets he could find. Brightly painted new homes had sprung up among the vine-covered shacks yet to be torn down, like zydeco irises in a field of dollar weed. As though pedaling through a graveyard, Myles did his best to keep to a respectful pace while trying not to be too obvious in his attempts to spot the professor's trailer in the back lots.

People looked up from their porch activities to see the out-of-place white dude on the bicycle. An old man pushing a lawn mower in a futile attempt at taming the four-foot weeds in a vacant lot let the gas motor die out. "Can I help you?"

After a morning of trying to describe the professor's rig, Myles had shortened his inquiry to the bare minimum. "I'm looking for a friend of mine. He pulls a circus-like trailer behind his bike. Last anyone saw of him, he was headed this way."

"Haven't seen him. If he was trying to escape someone, he probably headed away from the river."

"Why would you assume that?" Myles asked.

"Not many people come over here unless they're gawking or running." Covered in sweat, the man gave the pull cord a hard yank to restart the rattly engine.

"Thanks." Myles doubted he'd been heard, but politeness needed to be expressed even if the courtesy wasn't always acknowledged.

Though the streets had the same names as those that ran through the Quarter and the Bywater, the expensive neighborhoods on that side of the canal made the road signs in the Lower Ninth Ward seem like cruel jokes. Over ten years had passed since the flood, and walls and doors still bore the additions of large spray-painted X's and numbers referring to how many dead had been found by rescue teams.

He stopped at a yard that looked to be slowly devouring a handful of broken-down cars. Fresh tracks cut through the tall grass to a shed out back, which housed a brightly colored trailer.

He was in no condition for confrontation. Strangers poking around supposedly empty properties had a way of being greeted by gun-toting neighbors. Professor Yates had possibly taken refuge with a friend and parked his gear out back, but Myles wasn't hopeful as he approached the water-stained front door.

An old woman across the street yelled from her rocking chair on her porch. "There's no one home, mister."

"Any idea who dropped off that trailer out back?"

She returned to snapping her garden peas. "I don't want no trouble. He seemed to be a nice old guy."

Myles pushed his bicycle across the street to talk to the woman without the whole neighborhood listening in. "He's a friend of mine. I'm worried about him. Anything you can tell me would help."

"A black van cut him off. Three, maybe four, guys jumped out and shoved him and his scientific equipment in the sliding door. Then they hauled his empty trailer out back. Me and my boy were having breakfast when we heard the commotion. I don't want no trouble."

Myles doubted he'd have done anything different in her shoes. Bravery only made sense if the numbers worked in his favor. An old woman and a child against four thugs didn't add up well.

"I understand," he said. "It's not like the police patrol out here on a regular basis."

The woman's laugh conveyed both warmth and sarcasm. "Child, they don't come out here for nothing."

He could see she wouldn't have any idea of where they were headed, so he was reduced to grasping at straws. "Did he seem to be hurt?"

"Those guys were on him before he had a chance to get hurt. But I don't think he was what they were after. They gutted that trailer like they were stripping a BMW. I doubt you'd find a pocket calculator left in that wagon."

❧

WITH THE VERSATILITY of the bicycle, Myles was able to

double back numerous times on his ride from the Ninth Ward to the rental shop. Between the paranoia of believing he was being followed and the faces he'd seen repeatedly through the day, he grew suspicious of everyone. Dropping the bike off was nearly a relief. If someone was following, they'd either kidnap him or go back to being unnoticed in the shadows.

Kendell had suffered enough without having to endure more fear for his safety. He sneaked halfway up the stairs to her apartment. If anyone was on the street, he wouldn't see them, but if they checked the locked door to the street, he'd hear it.

Cheesecake, however, hadn't been consulted about the stealthy trap he'd set for any pursuer. She loosed a barrage of barking upon hearing him on the stairs. *It's not like they wouldn't know where I was headed.*

After the door to Kendell's apartment burst open, she stood at the entrance, glaring down at him. "Thank God you're okay. What were you thinking, sending a kid to warn me about you putting yourself in danger? And where is your goddamned phone? I told you to start carrying it with you. It doesn't do much good in the cushions of your couch." Her ire contrasted with Cheesecake, who stood at her side, smiling down at him.

Her concern warmed his heart. "Like you've never bolted into trouble without consulting me. You think maybe I forgot about you pulling out of my arms and jumping onto that paddle wheeler?"

Her attitude instantly changed. "Oh, yeah. I guess I'm not

going to live that one down anytime soon. Did you find the professor?"

He took her in his arms before entering the apartment. "I found his trailer. An eyewitness says he was shoved into a black van. His assailants took his equipment. Did you take a look at his map?"

"It's on the table. You think it might give us a clue as to what happened?"

Between fearing for his own personal safety and keeping an eye out for the professor, he'd had plenty of time to consider the options. He tore a piece of paper into little rectangles and drew a cartoon van on each. "The way I see it, there are three possibilities. This was a professional abduction, so for the moment, I'm leaving out any unknown operatives from the dark web." He drew a big *M* on the first slip of paper. "We know Colin Malveaux is out chasing Sanguine, but he can't be one-hundred-percent sure she has the walking stick. He's got the resources to hire a paramilitary force. Hell, he probably has his own."

"That doesn't make sense. He'd be better off following the professor and letting him do all the work. We know he doesn't have the cane."

Myles set the slip of paper on the Central Business District. "That's what I thought, too. But if they did take him, I'd expect they'd be holding him somewhere secure." He wrote a *P* on the second cartoon van. "That brought me to the police and the chief. I don't think Joe Cazenave is involved, but I do think the police are either keeping an eye on his activities or he's secretly still reporting to the chief. As a member of the Laroque family, the chief might be playing his own game." He put that cartoon van on the French Quarter police station.

Lines formed at the corners of Kendell's tightly closed lips. "Maybe, but we don't have enough to show for the chief to act so impulsively. I'd expect the police chief to wait until we've found something significant before moving in."

Finally, Myles jotted down *WTC* on the final slip. "That brings me to Luther Noire and that damn World Trade Center. He's got the resources. Again, I don't think Joe's guys are involved, but Luther could be keeping tabs on them or just getting the story firsthand from Joe. Luther is pretty sneaky. He knew the professor had modified his equipment. Look at all those *X*'s on the map. Those would look like pirate booty to Luther. If he's funding one secret force, why not two?" He drew a skull and crossbones flag atop the last van.

Kendell picked up Cheesecake so she too could inspect the map. "That would explain why they took both the professor and his equipment. The cane is just one enchanted object. With his equipment—once he was forced to tell them how to use it—they could scour New Orleans for all kinds of stuff."

He tossed the slip of paper onto a series of new circles and *X*'s that stretched out toward New Orleans East. "Suppose for a moment that the professor wasn't on the run but had gone to the Ninth Ward as part of his research. If he got some readings from the city, he'd need to triangulate the position of his finds."

"I might be able to make an educated guess. Six Flags has

been abandoned since Katrina, and being out in the elements, it's gotten run-down and overgrown."

Myles drew a question mark over the amusement park. "Great. Creepy clown ghosts."

"I'll round up the girls. They're not going to want to be left out of this search."

He hated his next idea, but he didn't know when they'd get their next chance. "You shouldn't come along."

She gave him the hard-eyed stare he'd grown accustomed to that said, *Try and stop me.* "Please don't pull that macho bullshit on me. You're not good at it."

"This isn't my desire to keep you safe. Actually, it's the opposite. We laid out this plan to figure out who was following us. With the professor captured and me and the band headed to the abandoned amusement park, we should have every potential pursuer on our tail. That will free you up to head out to the swamp to meet Sanguine."

Kendell was able to see the rational choice, which was one of the things he admired most about her. "You would be leading them in the opposite direction. I don't suppose a swamp witch would have much use for a car, so someone would have to go get her. And with Colin still on her tail, I'd be able to keep track of him. You know, you have your moments of brilliance."

"You'd be on your own. I wouldn't even trust telling Joe. In fact, I'm going to need him to run interference with any police that might be patrolling the wreckage of the park. If he got wind of your escapade, he'd insist on providing protection."

He could tell she was still analyzing the plan. "Colin's out of the way. Polly and the band will be searching the park, so that will bring along Joe and his team. You could be facing a problem if Luther is using someone from that team as an informant, but that would only ensure you'd have all of their attention. Didn't Charlie tell you we could borrow his truck? I can use that to drive out to the swamp. The only unknown would be if Colin has his own paramilitary force, but even if he does, they'd likely be following the action at the park. You really can be inspired at times."

"Two compliments in five minutes. That must be some kind of record. Just be careful. The only person unaccounted for in this little adventure is Madam de Galpion. I still don't trust that voodoo priestess. You could be stepping into a trap."

～

MYLES WINCED when Minerva's vintage VW bus let out a loud backfire as she shut it off in the otherwise empty Six Flags parking lot. It wasn't the most discrete of vehicles, but it had the advantage of being seen as a goth-hippie mobile. Any security guard who managed to catch Myles and the four women of the band would probably let the *crazy kids* off with a warning.

The authorities weren't what worried Myles, though. They'd have trouble subduing Cheesecake, let alone an unknown number of paramilitary dudes.

"I just want to see if they're holding the professor here," he said. "The idea is still to keep anyone following us distracted. Kendell said she needs at least two hours to get

Sanguine back to New Orleans. If any of you ends up in trouble, just give up. If nothing else, we can keep whoever is after us busy standing guard."

The band answered in unison, sarcastically. "Right."

Polly leaned over the back of the bench seat in front of Myles. "You're very sweet to look out for us, but you don't honestly think we're going to roll over and play dead, now do you? We're *women*, you fool. Maybe *you* should just stay in the bus."

"All I'm saying is don't get hurt. We don't need to fight our way out. Even if they have the professor captive in there, I don't think they'll hold him once they have what they want—or find out it's not here. He's more useful on the hunt than as a hostage."

Polly flipped her long blond hair at him as she turned back to the front and the creepy amusement park outside the windshield. "Whatever, dude. We intend on having a little excitement. They're not going to shoot us. That would just be stupid. So what's the harm in running around in a bunch of decaying fun houses?"

Myles could see a lot of harm, but then he'd never been big on carnival rides. "Okay. Back here in two hours?" He hoped making it a question would defuse their resistance to his apparent attempts at taking charge.

"Sounds good," Polly said. "We should pair off. Minerva and Scraper can take the north end of the park, and Lynn and I will take Myles to scope out the south end."

The park was every bit as disturbing as he had imagined. Gates hung open as if to say, *Enter if you dare.* Graffiti typically annoyed the crap out of him, but as the only indication that living, breathing, humans had survived their illegal exploration of the haunted park, he accepted the tagging as markers of past progress.

Lynn leaned in next to him. "I did a little research. You'll want to stay clear of the lakes and tall grass marshes. Alligators, snakes, and wild boars have taken up residency here."

Thanks for that. As if I didn't have enough to worry about. "At least I'm not seeing much in the way of security."

"Is that a good thing?" Polly asked.

"I'm not sure. I know this place is usually pretty well patrolled. I'd guess that means the thugs are associated with the cops—that would mean either Luther's men or the chief of police."

Lynn grabbed his hand and ducked behind a concession stand. "We're not alone."

The three of them pressed their backs against the painted plywood. Polly wrinkled her nose. "What is that disgusting smell?"

Lynn pointed at the Sno Ball sign they were leaning against. "Dead nutria marinated in fermented flavored sugar syrup and swamp water, probably with a side of bugs."

"I may never eat carnival food again."

Other than the buzz of some overactive mosquitoes, Myles didn't sense any threat. "What did you see?"

Lynn pointed at the source of the sound. A small, black drone was bobbing side to side. Before he could stop her, Polly bolted out from cover and hurled a rock at the aerial device. It came crashing to the ground.

Lynn rushed out to join Polly. "Good shooting, Tex."

"It's not the first time I've had one of these nerdy things spy on me. It probably didn't do much good, though. I'm pretty sure it saw us."

Myles picked up the drone and saw the rock had cracked the camera lens and bashed one of the propellers. "It's not police issue, but it's too sophisticated for a kid's toy. We're being watched, for sure."

"Another tick in the Luther Noire column," Polly said. "I'm beginning to really dislike that guy."

Myles pulled the batteries out of the drone just to make sure they weren't being heard. "Where there's one, there's bound to be more and, I'd guess, a mobile remote-control station as well. Has anyone spotted Joe's team? I thought they were keeping pretty close tabs on you guys."

Polly pulled out her phone. "I texted Joe we were headed out here on a lead. He said his team would be five minutes behind us."

Myles was doing his best to keep all the different possibilities straight, but without his map and cartoon vans, that wasn't easy. "If Joe told Luther, we may be headed into a trap."

"My impression is Joe plays his cards close to the vest," Polly said. "Based on how his team played zone coverage while they were watching us, I can tell they're a tight-knit group. Dudes like that don't share information with people they don't completely trust."

He had to admire her ability to understand the male psyche. "Just the same, we need to watch our backs. Any word from Minerva and Scraper?"

She continued staring at her phone. "They've found the

black van. It's near the old voodoo volcano ride in the boneyard. Anyone know what that ride looks like?"

Lynn pointed toward a tower of twisted metal. "How can you have grown up here and not ridden the volcano?"

Polly stashed her phone away. "I was usually busy behind the arcades, making out with some guy. Let's get moving."

Walking through Main Street Square was like witnessing a post-apocalypse vision of New Orleans. Originally designed to present a family-friendly, Disneyesque image of the often-seedy French Quarter, the abandoned, graffiti-covered buildings were even more frightening than the real thing.

Myles kept checking the sky for another drone. "We'd better keep under the balconies. Even though they know we're here, they may not know which way we're headed."

Lynn kept close to his side. "All this place needs is a horde of rampaging zombie clowns."

Myles's nerves were already on edge. Feeling a hand at the back of his shirt collar, however, convinced him that Lynn's assessment had come true. Another hand covered his mouth to prevent his none-too-manly scream from alerting the rest of the park. He and the two women were dragged into the Main Theater, which from the scattered chairs and refuse, looked to have endured its own private hurricane inside the structure.

The man dressed in black from head to foot whispered in Myles's ear. "Keep quiet. We're with Joe Cazenave. We're here to protect you."

The assurance of rescue instead of kidnapping calmed only Myles's brain. His heart didn't appear to appreciate the difference as it continued to pound much too quickly. "You guys are a little late."

Joe stood just inside the main entrance, surveying the street. "You weren't our first priority. If one of you would have mentioned we were up against another team of professionals, I'd have brought more men."

Myles calmed down at seeing Joe. "I wasn't sure who to trust. Our best guess is this team is from Luther Noire. Since you work with him, even telling you we were on this mission was a risk."

Joe took the news as stoically as ever. "I maintain a balance with Luther and Gerald. Neither want details about my activities, only results. The first thing we need to do is get Minerva and Scraper out of the action. Then my team can move in and rescue Professor Yates."

Polly already had her phone out. Her fingers moved lightning fast over the display. "They'll keep clear, but I'm not telling them where to go, just in case things get jinky."

"It's the professor's equipment they're after," Myles said, "and any paranormal artifact they found in the park that led them all here. But you're not going to get the professor out of here without his stuff, and I don't think he's going to trust another paramilitary force swooping in."

"Right. You're coming with me," Joe said. "While my guys are distracting the other team, you and I will get the professor and his equipment."

Myles hadn't intended to volunteer, only to clarify that simply grabbing the professor wasn't going to be very easy. "Then what? Run like hell? Wouldn't it be easier to disable the enemy?"

"Sure, if we knew who they were, how many of them there are, what kind of weapons they have, who they—"

"I get it. We don't want to add a bloodbath to the ambiance of this place. He'll probably have his equipment in the van. The professor doesn't travel light."

Joe nodded to his team before turning to Polly. "Once the action starts, round up your bandmates and hightail it out of here in the VW. We can use your escape as part of our distraction. Myles and I will steal the other team's van, so you should have a decent head start."

"What about the rest of your guys?" Lynn asked.

"They'll sneak out the same way we snuck in."

Back out in the street, Myles realized how little he knew about covert missions. Joe moved from shadow to shadow, avoiding any direct path toward their objective. Finally, he hunkered down behind a vine-covered turnstile.

"We'll wait here until my team makes their move," Joe said. "The van is fifty yards ahead and to the left of us, on the other side of the roller coaster. There will be at least one guard on the professor, but as they've all come in the same vehicle, I doubt there will be more than one. If we're lucky, he'll poke his nose out once the girls start up that jalopy. But even if he doesn't, I have ways of making him show himself. While I'm taking care of him, you make sure the professor is okay. I suppose it'd be too much to hope you know how to hot-wire a van."

Myles had owned his fair share of run-down vehicles with busted keys. "Not one like that."

"Just expose the wiring and fuses. Once I deal with the guard, I'll have that black beast running in no time."

A loud explosion preceded enough shouting to rival a rebel yell at a Civil War reenactment.

"That'll be our cue," Joe said. "Stay close behind me."

Myles wondered what use a frontal assault would be on a well-trained abduction team, but figuring out Joe's strategy wasn't his problem—getting through the thick brush without getting bit by a snake or alligator was. The man dressed in black moved so effortlessly through the tangled vines and bent metal he made Myles feel like a toddler crawling after his dad. Finally, the weeds that had done their best to trip him gave way to a blacktop service road.

After all the work getting through the bushes, Joe moved like an Olympian sprinter with the open van door as his finish line. Myles didn't even see the guard there until Joe had him pinned to the ground.

Feeling like the stupid kid brother who'd forgotten his part, Myles started running toward the van. The men were still struggling on the ground as he stepped around them and entered the vehicle.

The professor kept futzing with his equipment until he saw Myles. "About time someone showed up. I was running out of excuses about why I hadn't found anything out here."

"You're the expert on electronic equipment. Think you can help me hot-wire this van?"

"Stand aside." Professor Yates's fingers moved through the wires under the dashboard with such skill that Myles suspected that wasn't his first time.

After the van kicked over, Joe closed the sliding door. "It

was one of Luther's guys. I tied him up. Did you actually find anything out here, or was it all just a game?"

Professor Yates relinquished the driver's seat to Joe. "There's plenty of stuff out here worth finding but nothing that would warrant this level of activity."

endell fidgeted like a girl who'd just asked her father to let her use the family car as Charlie pulled his keys out of his pocket.

"You're sure you don't want me to come with you?" he asked. "Jenny can be a little persnickety with someone she doesn't know behind her wheel."

The battered red truck parked on the street looked as though it hadn't moved in months. "Myles and I need you here," Kendell said. "You're our backup in case something goes wrong."

"Your call. Pump the accelerator twice before you turn the ignition. If she doesn't start, don't touch the gas again until she does. You need to show her who's boss sometimes."

He stood next to the truck until she had it running, though she wasn't sure if his presence was for her benefit or to make sure the truck didn't have a hissy fit. He remained on the curb as she drove down the street and made a turn away from the Quarter.

She liked her little yellow scooter for traveling around town. It was cute and made her look sexy as hell in her short skirts. Charlie's truck sucked. The red Chevy was older than she was. It announced every bump and pothole with an ominous rattling of the suspension. The only looks she got behind the wheel were either from women glaring at her due to the noise or creepy men waiting for it to break down so they could swoop in and offer to help the damsel in distress.

Bad as the vehicle was around town, getting it up onto the freeway took all of her and the truck's combined willpower. She stepped hard on the gas, hoping nothing was about to burst out of the hood and pushed on the steering wheel in an attempt to get the rickety beast up to speed. At sixty-five miles per hour, she eased off and settled back onto the vinyl bench seat.

At least traffic wasn't bad on a Saturday for the half-hour drive out to the bayou. By the time she found her exit, her hands had built up a slippery layer of sweat on the hard steering wheel, but she and the truck had come to something of an understanding regarding who was driving and who should be responsible for propulsion.

She could practically feel the truck sigh with relief as she turned into a gravel parking lot and shut down the grumbling engine. *Don't get too comfortable. You still have to get me back home.*

She looked around the small lot to make sure she was alone. Feeling more than a little self-conscious, she put on the glasses and draped a blanket over her head. "Sanguine, are you close? I'm at the parking lot."

Though her face didn't appear in the glasses, Sanguine's message came in loud and clear. "I'm on my way. Just have to put a few more moves on Colin to get him good and lost in the swamp. Were you followed?"

Kendell mentally kicked herself for not being more observant, though driving the truck had occupied all of her attention. "I don't think so. Myles and the band are putting on a pretty good deception."

"I'm putting everything in your hands. You'd better not fuck up."

Though Kendell's first reaction was to make a snarky response, she had to agree. With all the work everyone had put in, though—plus the danger Myles and the band were enduring—the last thing she needed was a witch with cold feet. "Between a swamp witch and a voodoo priestess, we can handle anything thrown at us."

"Just be ready for me. I want to get to New Orleans and then back out here as fast as possible. The storm's getting closer."

Kendell took the makeshift hood off her head and scanned the area. She didn't see any signs of human activity. The trucks and trailers in the lot wouldn't be reclaimed until the fishermen returned from their day on the water. Every car that slowed down on the freeway overpass made her tense with fear. Though not a cloud was in the sky, the weather could change in an instant.

Nervously, she ran to the edge of the parking lot and peered along the winding river that cut through the swamp.

With a sigh of relief, she finally made out a small canoe working through the weeds. She started praying the truck would start.

The woman paddling the boat was far more muscular than Kendell had envisioned, but she'd only seen Sanguine's face across the glasses' communication link. In mud-caked jeans and a tank top so drenched in sweat her lack of a bra was obvious, she reminded Kendell of a woman escaping from a chain gang in some sexploitation movie. After beaching the canoe, Sanguine pulled a long cloth-wrapped object from the bottom of the boat.

"Is that it?"

"No. It's a smoked water moccasin. I thought I'd need a bite to eat on the trip to town. Of course this is it."

Kendell never had been a fan of sarcasm. "You don't have to be so snippy *all* the time."

"Sorry. A week in the swamp, living off the land while being pursued—especially since I had to lead him along— makes me grouchy. There's nothing worse than an unskilled adversary."

Kendell knew if their positions were reversed, she would have been far less amiable. She turned toward the truck, but the sound of ATVs made her stop cold. They came sliding to a halt, blocking the exit.

Shit.

As soon as the sound of the screaming engines died down, she heard the even-more-ominous high-powered airboat.

Sanguine was sprinting toward the truck. "Fuck! We're going to have to make a run for it."

Kendell tried to run, but her feet slipped on the gravel, and she fell to the ground. "Take the cane and go!"

Sanguine barely got the truck door open before the menacing airboat flew up the boat launch with Colin standing on the bow like a Viking warrior. The truck engine spun but refused to start.

They were outnumbered and trapped, but that didn't seem to be a deterrent for Sanguine. She jumped back out of the truck and tore at the cloth wrapping the cane. She pulled the staff out as if it was a high-powered sniper rifle. "Get back, or I swear to my gods I'll use this thing on all of you."

Colin jumped from the airboat with all the arrogance of a general whose men had just secured a beachhead. He shook his head as he stared at Kendell. "About time you came to rescue her. Did you really think I'd be so foolish as to try and capture the swamp witch on her own territory with nothing more than a leaky rowboat?"

"You want it?" Sanguine said. "You're going to have to pry it from my dead hands, and even then, you'll have a fight. This stick doesn't obey you any longer."

Colin motioned to his goons. "Empty threats? I expected better after all that time playing cat and mouse in the swamp. You really did a skillful job of keeping me on the hunt. Of course, having Kendell come to your rescue was a monumental mistake. I'm curious—why didn't you entice me so far out into the cypress grove I couldn't find my way back? Even with my GPS, I found returning to your grandmother's shack dicey a time or two."

Sanguine had the wild look of a cornered panther. "Ask

Kendell. I would have been more than happy to let you die out there. Listening to her is a mistake that will forever haunt me."

Even dirty and ragged, he maintained the aristocratic attitude that both revolted and enticed Kendell. "So I have you to thank for my life. I've said it before. We'd make powerful allies."

Kendell wanted to spit in his face, but the time for direct confrontation had passed. "I promise you, saving your life is a mistake I won't make a second time."

His self-important smile made her want to vomit. "Get in the airboat, both of you."

Sanguine still hadn't let go of the cane. "Why?"

"Thanks to Kendell's boyfriend, I now have Marie Laveau's diary regarding this stick. With Delphine's help, we're all going to see if we can get that damn silver head off and release the cane's full power. I never should have let that old voodoo queen convince me to let her put it on in the first place."

Sanguine kicked hard at the guards trying to manhandle her. She refused to let go of the cane, choosing instead to bite the arms of the men wrestling her to the ground. Kendell admired the hell out of the woman.

KENDELL HAD plenty of time on the noisy ride to gather her questions for Sanguine. When the boat finally docked, they were at a lavish house on the north shore of Lake

Pontchartrain, far from the constant activity of New Orleans—and far from those Kendell relied on for help.

As the two guards escorted Kendell and Sanguine off the boat, Colin led the way. "You'll be locked up in one of the bedrooms until Delphine arrives. Do what I ask, and we can all part amicably. Fight me, and things won't be nearly as pleasant."

Sanguine continued to hold the cane tightly. "Fat chance." She was unceremoniously shoved into the bedroom.

Kendell didn't see any point in wasting her energy resisting. She waited until the door lock clicked before turning to the young swamp witch. "Isn't getting the silver skull off the cane what we want? Can't Baron Samedi materialize—or whatever he does—and take it back to Guinee?"

Without her adversaries present, the other woman's energy evaporated. She collapsed on the bed like a little girl. "It's not that simple. We needed to get the cane away from Colin before removing the lock. Marie's spell did hold the cane in the physical world, but it also prevented the powers from the netherworld from being used here. If we remove the spell while Colin's holding the cane, he'll have control over those powers."

"What about Baron Samedi?"

She sat up and held the cane up for Kendell's inspection. "Ownership doesn't mean the same thing in the afterlife that it does here. Right now, you might think I own this stick because it's in my hand, but it won't respond to me. Through magic and trickery, Baron Malveaux stole this cane from Baron Samedi. That gave him some powers when it came to the afterlife, but not this life. Removing the lock while the cane is in Colin's possession will give him its full powers. But Baron Samedi isn't going to take that change sitting down. Colin's back among the living, and Samedi's back at the seventh gate—for now."

"So you're saying there will be another conflict?"

Sanguine turned the silver skull so it looked as though she was addressing it. "Should the two decide to duel it out, yes. But all that assumes we can get this thing off. Colin said you found a book?"

Kendell was still working her way down her list of questions. "I wanted to ask you about that. I could only open the front cover. It talks about you and I being the people who can remove the spell, but under the supervision of Delphine. The rest of the pages seemed like they were glued together."

"Did you try singing to it?"

Kendell didn't think it was the time for jokes. "Why on Earth would I do that?"

The look Sanguine gave Kendell again made her think of a snarky sibling. "That voodoo bitch didn't tell you? My gods, you two must be simple. Think, Kendell. Why would you sing to it?"

In a flash of insight, she understood what Sanguine was saying. "Madam de Galpion casts spells through smell. That's her special skill. I'm a musician. So you're saying that's how I express my power—through music?"

"How could you *not* know that?"

Though Kendell loved learning, being lectured annoyed

the hell out of her. "So what would happen if I started singing to the cane?"

"How the hell should I know? Wicca isn't voodoo. We don't cast hexes and go looking to the afterlife as the source of our power. Nature is my religion. What I do know is you don't go playing with magic without first knowing how to use it."

"For someone who keeps saying she's not a practitioner of voodoo, you do seem to know a lot about it. I've only been involved for a little while. A year ago, I was just a barista at a small coffee shop."

Sanguine slid up the bed to sit against the pillows stacked against the varnished pine wall. "A year ago, I was a sophomore at Tulane studying botany. That was before you started messing with the Malveaux curse. Once my grandma noticed the activity, she called me back to the swamp to teach me about my familial obligation."

Kendell sat at the edge of the bed. "I thought you'd always lived in the swamp."

If Sanguine had a snarky response, she didn't express it. "Of course I knew about my grandmother the swamp witch, and I spent a lot of my youth out there with her, learning about nature. She wanted me to get an education. I guess that's going to have to be on hold for a while."

"Is that why you hate me?"

For the first time Kendell could remember, Sanguine smiled. "You should talk to some of my past lovers. I'm at my most disagreeable with those I care about. My grandmother could see the future like waves on the ocean. Sometimes, a small undulation in the deep water can become a towering crest close to shore. She told me my life would be extraordinary, but even she didn't know how that would play out. You're the undertow that makes me rise up. Never think that I hate you."

Kendell had known Sanguine would make a powerful partner. "We need a plan."

"Yep, and it needs to be better than the last one because that's not working out so well."

~

MYLES SAW the flashing blue and red lights in front of his apartment as Joe missed the turn. "What the hell?"

Joe kept driving straight. "I don't know what they want, but it can't be good. And I'm driving a stolen van. Is there somewhere I can drop you and the professor while I figure out what's going on?"

"Take me across Rampart." Myles hoped they were early enough to catch Charlie at home.

Unfortunately, passing from the Quarter to the Treme didn't provide the relief Myles had hoped to find. A tow truck was dropping off Charlie's beat-up truck.

Myles barely waited for Joe to stop the van before he launched out the door. "Please tell me that damn thing broke down and Kendell is in the house."

"Sorry, man. I really wish that were the case. When she didn't get back, I got worried. Fred here's a buddy of mine who patrols the highway along the spillway for stranded motorists. I had him take a look. He found the truck but nobody with it. From the marks in the gravel, it looks like she had company, and not the type she expected. The truck door was open and the key in the ignition."

Myles turned back to Joe. "It has to be Colin's men. Any idea where they'd take her?"

He jumped from the front seat and glared at Myles. "First things first. What was Kendell doing out there? I thought we had an agreement that we'd discuss plans before running off on some half-baked idea. I can't provide protection if I don't know what's going on."

Myles could see he was more than perturbed. "Nothing personal, but someone told Luther Noire about the professor's equipment. I'd bet my tips for the night that they've been following the professor around, waiting for their opportunity to strike. I couldn't be sure telling you what Kendell was up to wouldn't result in exactly this same situation but with different players."

Joe uncrossed his arms. "Smart. Don't trust anyone you don't have to. How bad is the situation?"

Beyond Kendell once again being in danger, Myles hadn't considered what was at stake. "They would have waited until Sanguine showed up. That means they have the walking cane."

"Do they have the book?"

Myles stared at Joe, assessing what he might know. "How do you know there's a book?"

"Isn't there always some diary from Marie Laveau that has all the answers?"

Myles wasn't buying it. "Sure, but you weren't asking in general terms. What do you know?"

"You have your research libraries, and I have mine."

Joe would've had access to Luther's secret material. The man's office rivaled Delphine de Galpion's voodoo library.

"Our plan was for Kendell and Sanguine to use the diary to release the cane," Myles said. "Then with my connection to Guinee, we were going to have Baron Samedi come and take it back."

"Who has the book now?"

Myles's throat went dry. "Madam de Galpion."

"That's not good," Charlie said. "She was the first place I tried when I heard from Fred about the truck. Her car is missing from out back of her place."

Professor Yates had been quietly listening from the open sliding door. "I've got my equipment here in the van. My guess is they're all long gone from New Orleans. The good news is there are only a couple of ways out of town, and with them picking up Kendell on Highway 55, we'd have to assume they were headed north. I know it'll be like hunting for a stick in the forest, but it's the best I can come up with to find her."

Charlie didn't even bother checking on his truck before heading for the open sliding door of the van. "I'm coming with you. If there was ever a group that needed a bartender, it's one made up of a paramilitary dude, a crazy professor, and a guy who thinks he can hear voices in physical objects."

13

A long black 1970s Cadillac peppered the bedroom window with gravel from the driveway. Like a daughter waiting for her mom to get home, Kendell peered out between the curtains. Delphine slammed the car door as though pissed and stomped up the walkway to the front door.

Once the door opened, Delphine yelled loudly enough to be heard by everyone in the house, "I told you to leave her out of it!"

Colin's response was also pitched so that everyone could hear. "So long as everyone does as I ask, you'll all be free to leave this house at the end of the day, unharmed."

At the sound of the bedroom door being unlocked, Sanguine jumped off the bed with the cane still in her hand. "Time for us to get to work."

Kendell wished she'd had some way to practice her

newly revealed skills, but at least she no longer saw herself as a pawn in the high-powered game.

The guard motioned for them to move to the living room. In the middle of the elegant but comfortably furnished room, Delphine stood in her defiant stance in front of Colin.

The man had clearly gotten a shower and once again wore his old-fashioned suit. "Now that we're all here, I'll lay out what I want."

Sanguine clutched the cane to her chest like a cherished pet. "Whatever you have in mind, you can count me out. Your goons might wrestle this stick from me, but I'll never open its powers to you. I'll die first, and you know that's true."

"I expected some resistance. Delphine knows firsthand what I can do. Though she may not like my methods, she doesn't dare cross me. Kendell may still be discovering the extent of my powers, but she's suffered enough to know I'll stop at nothing. But you, Sanguine, hardly know me at all, except for the ghost stories your grandmother might have told you. I no longer have the powers over the dead as I once did—and will again—but there are conditions worse than death." He turned toward a black box on an end table. "Television on, weather channel. Leave the sound off."

Above a grand fireplace that took up an entire wall, a TV larger than Kendell's apartment came on. The hurricane it showed took up most of the Gulf of Mexico.

"It's bigger than Katrina," Colin said. "The reports are saying they don't even have a scale sufficient to categorize it. Most of Louisiana, from the gulf to the floodgates, will be wiped out. And we all know how unreliable any form of protection is when nature shows her hand, don't we, Sanguine?"

She turned as pale as her sandy-blond hair. "You couldn't have caused the storm—so this isn't a threat—that must mean you think you can stop it."

"Not on my own. I'm betting there are instructions in that book that will enable those of us in this room to at least influence its direction. But we'll need the power of the cane first. New Orleans is my home and base of power. The last thing I want is to see it flooded again. I just wanted you to see that we have a shared purpose."

Sanguine turned from the reporter's look of terror to the room's picture window and the clouds on the horizon. "And if I say no?"

"Dying is easy. Watching everyone and everything you care about get washed out to sea—and knowing you alone could have prevented it—will leave you a life filled with regrets. I'm not asking you to join me, only to see that, for the moment, we have a shared obligation."

The swamp witch's knuckles turned white as she squeezed the cane. "I'll go as far as reading the diary, but if there isn't some specific spell to combat that monster, I won't help you."

"That's a good girl. Kendell, you have the power to open this book."

His patronizing voice made Kendell wish Sanguine would hit him over the head with the cane. "I don't have the foggiest idea of how to unstick those pages." Her opening gambit held the advantage of partial truth, just in case anyone had the ability to detect such things.

Delphine pulled the book out of her oversized purse and set it on the coffee table. "You have to sing to it."

So you knew all along and didn't tell me. Once again, I'm going to have to apologize to Myles. Thank God he's smart enough not to rub it in. Kendell refrained from commenting, but her trick had confirmed Sanguine's suspicion that Kendell wasn't being taught what she needed.

Colin motioned toward the stereo system. "I know it's not the same as a live band, but this is a smart house. Just ask, and it'll play anything you like."

Kendell had had time in the bedroom to consider her choice, but she took a moment anyway. "House, play 'Diary of Jane' by Breaking Benjamin." Then she closed her eyes and sang along.

She'd experienced the power of an audience while standing on stage with her band at the Scratchy Dog. Performing while handling a cursed object from the baron had given her a feeling of being amped up on some high-powered energy drink. Even playing with the golden pick from the loas of the dead was an energy she could identify. Standing without her guitar and relying on only her natural abilities—both mystical and musical—made her feel emotionally naked. No mystical force was propelling her—just the magic of music, which she'd known all her life. The power that built within her wasn't from an outside source. The only time she'd felt something similar was when Myles had taken her to the *deep waters*. She was sensing *her* connection to every living soul. It was her back door into Guinee.

No one in the room had the impertinence to interrupt her while the song was playing. When she opened her eyes again, she saw the book open on the table, but the releasing of the pages had only been the confirmation of her abilities. She gave Sanguine a single nod. Only the swamp witch would know Kendell had established her connection with the cursed items Colin Malveaux wore as part of his costume.

After an hour of intense study, the three women came to a consensus.

Sanguine looked over her list of ingredients. "I think this will do it. Most of the stuff you should be able to find in the herb section of any grocery store. The plants are going to be more of a challenge. Someone will need to find a good local nursery. Anyway, this is what I need." She handed the slip of paper to the guard towering over her.

He scanned the list. "A vanilla frosty and fries?"

"For the last week, I've been eating bugs, snakes, and pickerelweed. If I'm to perform the nature spell correctly, I need to be in the right frame of mind. That includes food." She turned to Kendell. "Anything you want?"

Kendell didn't realize until that moment how hungry she'd gotten. "I could go for a diet Coke and some chicken nuggets."

Sanguine turned to the guard. "Make that two orders of nuggets."

The man looked annoyed as he turned toward his boss.

Colin merely nodded. "I would kill for a burger so long as you're out."

"Right, boss." The guard fumbled for his keys.

~

"BUSTING ass across Highway 12 isn't the easiest way to read this equipment." Professor Yates had been complaining since they had left New Orleans.

Myles suffered both Joe's desire to move as quickly as possible to find the women and the professor's need to make sure they weren't missing something important. What he really wanted was to take Charlie up on his offer to play bartender, but alcohol didn't seem likely to help. "Joe, is there anyone you could talk to about what properties Colin Malveaux might have available for his use up here?"

"Only if you want to get caught. With the cops at your apartment, I don't dare contact my people in the department. We are still in a stolen vehicle."

Myles thought the reminder that they were on the lam, after the previous dozen, was unnecessary. "Yeah, and with our run-in with Luther's guys, I doubt they'd be any more helpful. This is their van."

"If you want to take over the driving, I can work some back channels. We probably won't discover much as I'd think Colin would want to use a place that wouldn't be easily discovered, but riches combined with arrogance have a tendency to make people careless."

After only a moment at a turnout off the freeway, they'd

switched seats. Driving the stolen van was more nerve-wracking than Myles had imagined. He was certain every cop that sped by was ready to cut him off and make a dramatic arrest. The well-marked exits for the college town of Hammond faded in the rearview mirror. Ahead, random, poorly marked turns off the freeway came upon Myles before he had a chance to read the signs. Dense forests of pine and hardwoods blocked any view of what might be going on in the small hamlets set back from the thoroughfare. Myles wouldn't see Kendell waving for his help, but seeing nothing but trees made the trip frustratingly slow. Each time he hit the gas, however, Professor Yates complained he wasn't able to get stable readings.

Joe crept forward and put his hand on the back of the driver's seat. "Margery Laroque has a boathouse outside Madisonville. That's Colin's mother. She's head of New Orleans Bank and Trust. The location is remote and right on the water. Since the women were abducted from the launch site, they might have been taken by boat. Charlie's friend said he found only the fresh ATV tracks there—no other vehicles."

Myles had been so worried about Kendell, he hadn't bothered to figure out how she'd been abducted, only by whom. "It's worth a shot. I can't just keep driving this freeway, hoping for some ping on the professor's equipment."

Once off the busy, well-traveled route and on a rural two-lane road, Professor Yates started to perk up. "Now we're talking. There's some energy source straight ahead. If we take a couple of side streets, I should be able to triangulate a position."

"Sorry, Professor, I'm not wasting more time wandering around when we have a lead on our destination. Keep checking your equipment to make sure I'm headed in the right direction, but other than that, I'm just going to rely on you for confirmation."

Keeping to the speed limit took all Myles's restraint. The last thing they needed so close to their target was to get pulled over by some small-town cop looking to fill his ticket quota.

The small town of Madisonville, with its historic, well-maintained homes and old-fashioned store fronts, exuded rural Louisiana charm. Unfortunately, the slow pace of life extended to the speed limits. Having to stop every block at stop signs only further infuriated Myles. Apparently, the city hadn't bothered to invest in street signals. As he turned onto LA-1077, he yelled back at the professor. "Are you sure I'm going the right way? This looks like a residential neighborhood, not a way out to the lake."

"The twists and turns through town have helped me zero in on a location. According to the GPS map, we're right where we want to be. A couple more blocks, and we should be free and clear of the town."

Once they'd passed the houses, with their neatly manicured yards, the native grasses on the sides of the road shot up higher than the roof of the van. Myles tried peering through the vegetation while he drove, but it effectively blocked out any homes that might have been sitting close to the water.

Joe pointed out a mailbox covered in vines. "I think that's it."

Myles slowed the van to a crawl in order to not miss the turn. Once on the gravel road, he continued to keep the vehicle down at the lowest speed possible until he found a turnout wide enough to park without being seen from the house. "Okay, Professor, time to impress me. I don't want to bust in on some sweet little old couple who happen to have a nice collection of antiques with powers they don't suspect."

Having taken the professor's class, Myles knew the man often bullshitted his way out of situations, but as Professor Yates stood up in the back of the van, he exuded a confidence that Myles had never seen in class. "This is it. Whatever is in that house isn't displaying any kind of energy I've ever seen before."

Charlie had been uncharacteristically quiet in the passenger seat. He pulled out his hip flask. "A quick sip of courage before entering battle?"

Myles had never in his life felt so happy to have a personal bartender along. "Is that rum?"

"I could hardly carry the whole bar inventory. I thought rum was the most apropos."

Myles snatched the narrow metal canteen from his friend. "Time to find out if we're going to get any help from the beyond." He jumped out of the van and ceremoniously poured a small libation on the ground for the ancestors. Then he used the flask's lid to offer a drink to the loa of the dead.

Baron Samedi rose up out of the ground where the rum moistened the gravel. "You found it?"

"It's not that simple. Colin Malveaux has Kendell and the new swamp witch."

The all-black irises in the center of his white eyes rotated to take in the compound, appearing to see more than just the obvious. "Madam de Galpion is also here with the spell book. If my enemy is able to remove the silver skull before I get my hands on the cane, it will be an all-out war between the living and the dead."

~

THE BITE TO eat helped Kendell focus, but Sanguine's herb concoction smoldering on the coffee table didn't mix well with the deep-fried chicken nuggets in Kendell's stomach. Singing while breathing in smoke wasn't a skill she'd ever had to master. In the early days of the Scratchy Dog, singers had to endure secondhand smoke filling the room, but no longer.

Delphine sat on the couch with the diary on her lap. "The secret is not to fight it. You have to fill your lungs with the smoke and let it work on your vocal cords. To break the spell requires Wicca and voodoo to act as one."

Instead of fighting the fumes, Kendell allowed them to fill her body and soul. Her awareness of her existence extended beyond her body until she encompassed the whole room.

Colin was sitting on the opposite end of the long leather couch from Delphine. He held the walking cane like some sort of demented potentate expecting to be endowed with all the powers of the afterlife. Kendell knew what she had to do. She and Sanguine had a plan. She wasn't going to completely give in to what Colin wanted, but if things didn't work out, that would be the end result.

The TV continued to show the growing storm. The predictions were that the citizens of the gulf coast had two days to get out of town. *Plenty of time*, Kendell told herself.

Summoning her memory and self-condemnation from her time with Robert Johnson, she turned to the house computer. "Play 'Sympathy for the Devil' by the Rolling Stones." As she sang along, she envisioned the words being not only about herself but also Colin and even the cane as well. The words came out of her mouth as puffs of smoke, darker and more concentrated than the light haze filling the room. Like ocean waves lapping the shore, dark ridges of vapor washed over the silver skull. The energy she expelled was soft and methodical. The knob wouldn't be forced off but enticed into submission.

Like a scientist observing an experiment, Delphine kept track of the energy holding the silver skull to the cane by rubbing her fingers over the diary pages and smelling the effect. "The counterspell is working."

Kendell felt a shift in power. The smoke from Sanguine's smudge pot heightened her connection to everyone in the room but dulled any stimulation from outside the walls.

A breath of cold, fresh air brought her back from the beyond. People were rushing in the open front door. *Myles.*

"Now, Kendell, do it now!" Sanguine's words refocused Kendell on the plan.

She was still connected to the cufflinks Colin wore—the small gold accoutrements that had belonged to the baron Malveaux and been cursed by Marie Laveau, one of them modified by Madam de Galpion to obey Kendell's demands. She lifted her arms wide like a person being crucified. Across the room, Colin Malveaux dropped the cane as he rose from the couch with his arms mirroring hers. The tiepin at his chest called out to her. All she had to do was turn it toward his heart and push it in like an entomologist displaying an insect.

She sensed more than saw the man standing in front of her.

"No, my dear," he said. "You are not a killer. Leave him to me."

All she could make out clearly through the haze was Baron Samedi's eyes. His dark features, even highlighted by the white skeleton markings, mixed in with the smoke, making him appear even more ghostly than normal. "Sanguine can stop the storm, but she needs the cane. You owe it to Myles to let her try."

Kendell maintained her stance as she watched the swirls of smoke that followed Sanguine as they rushed toward Colin. With her heightened awareness, she knew her friend had picked up the staff. The new swamp witch swung it once over her head like a cheerleader handling a baton and struck the book with the end containing the silver skull. It popped off into Delphine's lap.

An emerald-green light illuminated the haze over the end of the cane in Sanguine's hand. Where the hollow skull had been, a chunk of glowing rock remained. Fortunately, the girl didn't spend long admiring the new handle. She rushed toward the daylight of the open front door.

The men, including Myles, still stood around like zombies who weren't sure whom to attack.

Uttering the words, "Let her pass," took all Kendell's strength.

The last of her energy gave out, and she fell to the floor. When Colin was freed from Kendell's control, Baron Samedi rushed toward the man. The flurry of activity stopped at the sound of an engine firing to life and gravel being strewn from the tires.

"No!" Colin's voice filled Kendell's ears and soul.

The last thing she saw before passing out was the man and spirit running for the door.

MYLES WAS STILL TRYING to blink the sting of the smoke out of his eyes as he cradled Kendell in his arms. She'd only been knocked out for a few minutes, but that time felt like an eternity. He too easily recalled being under the baron Malveaux's possession and feared she'd suffered a similar fate.

"Well, that did not go as planned," he said.

She sat up but remained in his arms. "What happened?"

"Sanguine stole Delphine's Cadillac. Colin jumped in his SUV, with Baron Samedi in pursuit, to chase her. The guards hit the floor when you passed out. Joe and Charlie tied them up and have them locked in a bedroom. But those aren't our current problems." He nodded toward the TV.

"That storm that was supposed to be days away is barreling down on New Orleans like an attack dog that sensed an intruder."

Delphine came over and sat next to them with the book in her hands. The woman looked frazzled. "Like attracts like. The energies of the cane, Baron Samedi, and whatever Colin has going on in his joint soul are working on the storm like electromagnets."

Kendell sat bolt upright. "We have to get Cheesecake! The band! We have to go right now."

Myles shook his head. "Don't worry. I called Polly while you were unconscious. Minerva is already picking up everyone in her bus and will be headed this way as soon as she can. Getting Cheesecake was her first stop. What were you two thinking?"

"Sanguine knew a storm was coming, though she didn't say anything about it being the mother of all hurricanes. Her powers are based on nature. She figured that, with the cane, she could harness the energy of the storm and use it against Colin. We expected him to chase her."

At least Kendell hadn't joined in the pursuit, but Myles knew Sanguine being in danger would eventually suck Kendell back into the maelstrom. "So she's just going to head straight into the eye of a hurricane and hope that magic wand can knock some sense into Colin?"

"Our options seemed pretty limited. We couldn't separate the baron from Colin since they're now one spirit. Sending him to Guinee might start a war between the loas of the dead. And leaving him among the living only prolongs our struggle against him. Sanguine believes with enough energy she can create a Wiccan purgatory to isolate Colin."

"You foolish children," Delphine said. "The amount of energy required to create an alternate reality is staggering. By using the cane to gather that power, she'll be creating a whole new hell made up of both Wicca and voodoo. Did you consider that every afterlife has someone in charge? Even if he is alone, you'll be creating a god. And what if he's able to catch up to her and takes the cane while she's building her new reality?"

Myles felt as though his head was spinning. "What about Baron Samedi? He's not going to let her keep his cane. That would only replace Colin with Sanguine as its owner."

Delphine handed the book to Kendell. "So now we have a three-way battle for control of the cane going on in the middle of the worst hurricane New Orleans has ever seen. A storm, by the way, that doesn't feel completely natural in origin. If Baron Samedi does regain his staff, it's unlikely he'll care about stopping the hurricane. The dead don't spend much time worrying about the trials of the living. If Colin ends up with the cane, we may be facing a whole new type of devil. At the very least, we've released its power for his use. We had all better hope Sanguine knows what she's doing."

Kendell flipped through the book as though searching for an answer. "We tackle one problem at a time. Though my cynical impression is that Colin would sit back and watch the world burn, New Orleans is his home. If he ends up with it, I'm sure he'll do what he can to stop the storm.

What good is having power if there's no one left to boss around?"

Her constant attempts to put Colin in a less-than-evil light bugged Myles. "Sanguine's the only one we can really count on. She's read enough of the book to know how to use the cane to influence the hurricane's direction."

Delphine looked out the living room's bay window at the wall of black clouds on the horizon. "I hope you're right about Sanguine. At this point, we're at the mercy of that storm's desires. If it decides to march across the lake, there's nowhere we could run."

14

Colin's fury was matched only by the growing hurricane, which battered his Ford Expedition. Off in the distance through the worsening rain, the taillights of the vintage Cadillac were still visible. Being low to the ground, it didn't suffer the winds that rocked his SUV, but with each flooded section of road it hit, the possibility of water soaking the engine—and rendering the vehicle inoperable—made him push his truck a little harder.

"You're a damn fool. Any woman who crosses your path that you can't crush under your toe sends you into a fit of rage." Baron Samedi didn't so much sit as hover in the passenger seat.

"I'm only allowing you to tag along because we agree she should *not* use that cane. Once it's back in my hands—"

"Something I'll never allow to happen," Baron Samedi interjected.

"A battle for another time. The point is, if she uses it, we'll both be in a world of trouble."

Cars were filling the northbound lanes of the Causeway. The twenty-four-mile-long bridge across Lake Pontchartrain was the most direct—but also the most precarious—route out of New Orleans. Winds from the outer bands of the storm found free range across the wide-open water of the lake and plowed with full force into the narrow strip of raised cement and asphalt.

Each time the steering wheel pulled hard to the left, Colin swore and yanked it back in line with his quarry. Clouds darker than the black Cadillac filled the sky.

"Can't you just manifest over there and push her into the guardrail or something?" Colin asked.

"You know better than that. As a loa of the dead, I can only go where I'm invited. And without my cane—"

"Don't start again. I need all my anger to keep this damn vehicle from going over the side of the bridge."

When they'd finally put the two-lane causeway behind them, Colin expected Sanguine to make a turn toward the city. Cars jammed the interstate on-ramp headed out of town. With the evacuation order in place, all routes into the city would be severely restricted, both to save the lives of the fools who wanted a closer look and to provide more lanes of traffic for escape. That would be the perfect place to catch her.

Apparently, she had the same realization. Instead of joining the throngs of vehicles, she continued straight toward the eye of the storm.

"Would you look at that thing? The funnel must be

larger than the city's diameter." He hadn't meant to engage Baron Samedi in conversation, but the event proved too huge to not make a comment.

"You know she's trying to kill you." Even with the howling wind and rain hitting the SUV from the side, Baron Samedi's words came through loud and clear.

"She's tried before. You of all beings know I don't fear death."

"If she succeeds before one of us gets hold of that cane, you'll find your next visit to the unknown far less enjoyable than the last."

Despite the Ford losing more traction on the flooded streets, he hit the gas. "You're saying I'd be better off if you're holding the cane? I doubt that."

"If I don't have that cane, every being you wronged will be out to get you when you die. Trust me, I know. If she has her way, you might not even end up in Guinee."

Colin, as Baron Malveaux, had deposed Baron Samedi, but what had happened to the original loa of the dead in that supernatural exile had never crossed Colin's mind. "Where the hell do you think she's going?"

"*Hell* would be all too simple." Baron Samedi sat calmly in the passenger seat as though they were headed out for a day of fishing.

The long Cadillac made a couple of turns through a suburb filled with panicky people trying to shove too many belongings into too many cars. The turn toward the Huey P. Long Bridge, which crossed the Mississippi, nearly flipped Colin's truck. With each foot of incline up the bridge, the wind picked up by five miles per hour. Even the train that crossed between the north- and southbound lanes squealed at the unrelenting storm's attempts at toppling it into the river.

On the far side of the bridge, structures were suffering the more direct effects of the storm. Debris was interspersed with the driving rain.

To Colin's annoyance, Samedi continued to watch it all with indifference. "You're not making much progress on her. This truck is going to go flying into the marsh a lot sooner than that low-slung town car."

"What choice do I have?" Colin hated not having a plan. Nothing good ever happened from running after someone half-cocked.

She finally turned off what remained of the major road into the Jean Lafitte Preserve as the outer rim of the storm's cone blackened the roadway ahead.

"Great, another fucking swamp," Colin said. "I should have known."

The red brake lights of the Cadillac meant Colin had survived the chase, at least. The woman had no sense at all. He watched in disbelief as she got out of the car and climbed onto its roof. The wind should have carried her away, but with the cane in her hand, she looked to be commanding the storm.

"Get out of that SUV, you fuckface!" Her words, like those of Baron Samedi, carried clearly to him despite the deafening hurricane-driven winds.

He knew better. Baron Samedi wouldn't be affected by the storm, and apparently Sanguine had special powers with the walking stick. Colin was neither a supernatural being nor in possession of a magical wand, but he had an anger neither of the other two could match—one capable of defying even the giant hurricane. Without fear, he opened the truck's door, which was promptly grabbed by the storm and ripped from its hinges.

"That cane belongs to me!" he shouted.

"You want it? Go fetch." She turned away from him and flung the staff into the mouth of the hurricane.

In a panic, he chased after the stick, which rotated up and away from him. He lost his footing, but instead of falling, he sailed clear above the car and the deranged woman who laughed like some wicked witch who'd just trapped her prey.

He looked back toward the cane, not wanting to lose sight of his objective. With both hands, he reached toward it, not caring that he was being sucked into the storm. The hurricane carried them both in its vortex of fury, but if he could just grab it, he might gain control of even nature's elements.

The screeching of the storm sounded like the cackling laugh of on old woman. He looked beyond the staff at the vertical wall of rotating clouds, but it wasn't simply a mass of gray and black. He'd seen that face with lightning for eyes and a cavernous mouth before, but the old, blind swamp witch was now pure energy.

She screamed at him as if the hurricane-force winds were driving her voice. "I warned you that, if you became a rabid dog, I'd put you down. Welcome to my version of hell."

～

KENDELL HELD Cheesecake tightly in her arms. The logical solution would have been to tell the band to get as clear of the storm as possible and to take the pup with them. However, she couldn't stand the idea of being without her dog or, if the worst should happen, having her companion carry on without her. "You guys should get on the road if you're going to beat the hurricane."

Minerva plopped down on the couch. "Sure thing. Just as soon as my old bus has a chance to catch its breath. Air-cooled engines aren't designed for stop-and-go traffic. Hell, it gets hot just hauling our instruments around town."

Kendell wasn't about to let everyone put their lives in danger. "You have to at least try. Take the van Myles stole."

"Hey, now," he said, "I wasn't the only one doing the stealing. And that thing isn't set up for passengers. It was a snug fit with the four of us guys."

Polly made a point of using her finger to count each person in the room. "I count ten people and one dog—not including the guards you have locked in the other room. Tell me, Queen Solomona, who's to live and who sits here, waiting for the storm?"

Kendell wasn't going to let her band leader intimidate her—not when it came to life or death. "The professor, Myles, Joe, Delphine, and I are part of this mess. Though I won't speak for any of them, for my part, I can't run. Either my plan with Sanguine works and that storm moves off, or I'll accept the consequences. I'm sure Charlie would be happy to have one of you sit on his lap in the van. The five of you have to make a run for it."

The rabble of voices protesting Kendell's self-sacrifice made Cheesecake growl at those rude enough to contradict her mistress.

Professor Yates stood in the middle of the room and called for calm. "It isn't going to matter. With the speed of that hurricane, no one would be able to outrun it. Then there's the fact that all the roads will be clogged with people trying to escape, stranded cars, and all manner of the worst in humanity. Honestly, I'm surprised you made it here so fast. Looking at this house's construction, I'm thinking this may be one of the safest places to hole up. But if it comes down to the worst, I'd rather die with friends than be stuck fighting for survival."

Charlie had been fumbling with some piece of furniture along the wall. He turned toward the group with a couple bottles of tequila. "Then let's make it a party."

Joe Cazenave always looked to be on duty no matter the situation. For the first time Kendell could remember, the man looked at ease. "I'm not a fan of drinking while at work, but as there's nothing else to be done in this instance, I vote for music and margaritas."

Polly cranked up the house's sound system and spun around the living room as though she was on stage. Cheesecake, never one to let a lady dance alone, trotted out and barked along with the music. Each time Polly pointed at the pup, Cheesecake ran around in a tight circle.

The entertainment, however, failed to distract Kendell from the darkening skies. Somewhere toward the heart of the beast threatening to swallow New Orleans, Sanguine was tempting the devil. Kendell had never felt so helpless. Even putting on the glasses to warn her friend of the consequences of failure would only distract her from her mission. And so far, Sanguine had proved to be the smarter of the two. All Kendell could do was hope the plan in the swamp witch's head was more thorough than they'd discussed.

After an hour of entertainment, the power finally gave out.

Unfortunately, that left Polly with too much pent-up energy. "Let's play some music or something. I can't stand sitting around waiting to die."

"We're not going to die," Lynn said. "But I do like the idea of doing something. We have all the instruments. Minerva had the bus loaded up for the next gig before we made a run for it."

After only a couple of runs out to the bus in the pelting rain, all the equipment was inside. Even Cheesecake looked happy for the new distraction. She barked at each person who reentered the house then ran to the living room to show them where to set up.

Kendell sat on the couch and pulled Cecile from the white-fur-lined guitar case. She looked over at Myles, who was smiling and rubbing his fingers together. If ever there was a time to pull out the gift from Papa Ghede, this was that time. The golden guitar pick shone in the flash of a lightning strike.

Without electricity to power their amps, the women sat comfortably with the listeners instead of standing for their attention. Myles took a seat next to Kendell—Cheesecake at her feet—while she faced the window. Without consulting the others, she started strumming the opening to "Who'll Stop the Rain."

Within a handful of notes, Polly picked up on the tune. "That's how it's going to be, huh? Okay. We'll blow this hurricane back out to sea with our playing."

Everyone in the room joined in with her sweet voice.

They played, sang, and drank as night fell. Rain pelted the storm windows, but the house proved more substantial than a concrete bunker.

Kendell did her best not to shred yet another set of strings, but the restraint left her fingers tired. It'd been a long day. She set the guitar down and turned to Myles. "I imagine there are plenty of bedrooms in this place, but I think I'd rather just snuggle up with you and Cheesecake on the couch."

"I think we all might feel better in each other's company," Polly said. "I know the drill about moving to a windowless room of the house, but the hurricane doesn't seem to be moving any closer, and this room has held up without any issues."

Professor Yates waved his empty margarita glass at the window. "Hurricane-resistant laminate glass—you can tell from the reinforced heavy-duty steel frame. Someone sank a lot of money into making this place the perfect viewing room for any sized storm. I'd be willing to bet this house gets blown off its piers before those windows give out. And I ain't moving from this chair."

As if the professor's words were the validation everyone

was waiting for, the rest of the group settled into whatever pieces of furniture they found most comfortable.

Despite the threatening storm, Kendell was asleep in Myles's arms in a matter of minutes.

~

THE MORNING after the big storm held an electric energy for Kendell. Everyone in the room had come through it unscathed. She snuggled against Myles, who was still breathing so deeply she knew he was asleep. Cheesecake jerked her legs and let out little doggy barks, indicating she too was still lost in dreamland. Kendell didn't want to leave his subconscious embrace, but she also wanted to see what had become of the hurricane. Carefully, she unwrapped her body from Myles's arms.

She tiptoed between her bandmates, who'd crashed out on cushions scattered about the floor.

As she passed Professor Yates in the recliner, he whispered to her, "I found an emergency radio in the kitchen. They're calling it a weather anomaly. Their current best guess is that upper-level winds from the north blew the top off the hurricane and it just died out, but when meteorologists start using fancy terms, it usually means they have no idea what happened. Sounds to me like your friend succeeded in her mission."

The morning light turned the few scattered clouds every color from deep purple to bright yellow. "Any estimates of damages?"

"Nothing yet. Just the typical flooding and blown-out

windows, but nothing like after Katrina. Sounds like the new pump stations and storm walls did their jobs. Plaquemines Parish got hammered, but anything below the floodgates was bound to get the brunt of the storm surge."

What she really wanted to know was how Sanguine had made out, but she feared what she might see—or not see—if she put on the glasses. "I'm going out to the deck for a while if anyone needs me."

The recliner gave the familiar leather groan she remembered from her father's favorite chair as the professor leaned over the side. "No matter the ultimate outcome, everyone put in heroic efforts yesterday." He made it sound as though the attempt was all that mattered.

"I fear the battle might not be over."

He settled back into the chair. "Probably not, but the latest storm has passed—hopefully figuratively as well as literally."

The heavy sliding-glass door released its hold on the frame with a rush of air. The wooden plank deck was cold and wet under her bare feet. She looked along the dock, expecting to see the dreaded airboat that had carried them across the lake. Only frayed ropes remained. Out of curiosity, she walked along the wraparound porch until she spotted the overturned boat in the reeds neighboring the boathouse. The cage that protected the propeller had been badly mashed. A feeling of smug satisfaction swept over her as she eyed the wreckage.

The lake had the typical calm after a big storm. She looked across the water, trying to envision the situation in New Orleans. She wondered how many people were stranded without shelter and how many had been unable to escape in time. As a barista and musician, she could do precious little. Even as a practitioner of voodoo, her skills seemed woefully inadequate.

Polly, wrapped in a blanket, stepped out of the house. "I don't care if it is summer, hurricanes put a chill in my bones."

"I wish there was something we could do."

She leaned against the wooden railing next to Kendell. "You realize today is Friday?"

At first, the veiled suggestion of playing their usual gig at the Scratchy Dog struck Kendell as insensitive, but music and drink were two of New Orleans's go-to solutions to tragedy. Someone needed to get out there and play for the soul of the city. "We should head down as soon as possible. The club will probably need to be cleaned out. We'll also need to find a generator."

Polly motioned toward the garage. "I bet I know where we could find one."

"That's called stealing."

"Technically, after a storm, it's looting, but I doubt the Laroques are going to come after us for that."

The thought of being able to play so soon after a disaster quickened Kendell's pulse, but another issue was more pressing. "I need to find out what happened to Sanguine, but I can't bring myself to contact her. If she's dead, I don't want to know."

"People have a way of surprising you. Take Myles, for example. Don't tell him I said so, but that boyfriend of yours is pretty good at figuring things out. I'm still not sure how he managed to find you out here in the sticks."

Kendell turned back to the living room and saw Cheesecake stretched out along Myles's side, right where Kendell had slept. The scene tugged at her heart.

"He's one of the good ones," she said.

"I won't tell you not to worry about Sanguine, but she is a swamp witch. If anyone could weather a storm, I'd think it'd be her. I'm going to see if the professor can work up some scientific magic capable of brewing coffee. There has to be a camp stove or something around here somewhere."

Kendell pointed to the dusty cabinets. "Try above the stove. That's where I keep my emergency gear for when the power goes out."

People were stretching out of their sleep and showing signs of life in the living room.

Joe emerged from the garage and caught Kendell before she could rejoin the group. "I know you want to return to the city. Before we took off on this crazy adventure, there were squad cars at Myles's apartment. After last night's hurricane, the force will be busy keeping the peace, so whatever their beef was with Myles, it's probably on the back burner. I just thought you should know it's not the safest down there for either of you. Even if Baron Samedi's cane is no longer the target of everyone's larceny, there's still the Laroque family, the police force, and Luther Noire to contend with. Those problems didn't just get washed away."

She wished she hadn't needed the reminder. "Are you saying we should make a run for it?"

"No. I'm just pointing out that New Orleans after a hurricane isn't the most predictable of cities."

"What about you? We kind of trapped you between the police and Luther."

He took on the hard look of a soldier who'd seen too much action. "I've learned not to rely on any organization. I'll let my team know you're headed back to New Orleans. When I get back to the city, I'll figure out what's going on. If you see me back on the force, you'll know everything's returned to normal. In the meantime, you'd be better off not trusting anyone too much."

As she returned to the living room, Joe headed off down the driveway, talking on his clunky military-grade phone.

Polly had gathered the band together. "We're headed back to the city. We owe it to our fans to play tonight. The problem is we've only got Minerva's bus, and that will barely hold us, Myles, Cheesecake, and our gear. There's bound to be a lot of cleaning up to do before we can play."

Charlie was lounging in one of the big recliners as though he owned the place. "That leaves me, Professor Yates, Madam de Galpion, and Joe to follow along in Luther's van. We can bring anything that doesn't fit in your VW. And I'll wager you could use a good bartender or two tonight."

Professor Yates was attending to the camp coffee pot in the kitchen. "I don't have anywhere I need to be today. Not like anyone's going to want to have their fortune told. I'd be happy to have a look at the wiring."

Kendell figured Delphine would have her hands full, making sure everything in her voodoo back room hadn't exploded into some demonic cross-curse nightmare—not to mention all the perfumes that might have fallen from the shelves.

"I think I'll pass on the entertainment," the voodoo priestess said. "Someone needs to make sense of everything that's happened over the last few days. I'll probably need a whole new journal."

After a breakfast of whatever they could find in the kitchen, the band loaded their equipment into the VW.

Delphine pulled Kendell aside. She had the silver skull in her hand. "You did a lot of work to secure this. I thought you might want to keep it in a safe place."

Kendell turned the knob made from hammered pieces of eight in her hand. She didn't have Myles's ability to read an object's history, but holding something so highly impregnated with energy was like handling a dead rat— some things just had to be experienced to be understood. "Cheesecake has made it clear she doesn't want anything more to do with any object subjected to the Malveaux curse. I can't keep it at my place."

"Typically, I'd be the first to take the skull. After all, Marie was the one who cast the binding spell. But the diary was clear. It's yours as the Inheritor, as is the book itself. Store it with the baron's other old possessions. You never know when it might come in handy."

Kendell walked out into the morning light, staring into the hollowed-out eye sockets of the small sculpture. If she turned it just right, she could barely make out the old Spanish markings. She was so intent on the engravings she nearly ran into Minerva as the drummer was hauling part of her kit to the bus. "You're still holding Fleurentine Laurette-Malveaux's old trunks for me. Think you could add one more thing to her collection?"

Minerva took the skull and inspected the hole underneath. "Actually, if you think it wouldn't be too dangerous, it might make a nifty knob for my gear shift. My old bus can use all the help it can get."

15

The drive from the north shore to New Orleans took three times as long as normal after the storm. The challenge wasn't only the traffic, though plenty of cars were searching out the same circuitous route home, keeping the old VW bus company. With all the street flooding and poorly marked detours, getting back to the city was like following a series of secret clues to an exclusive rave.

Myles wasn't a fan of Minerva's vintage bus. Every time the engine sputtered from sucking in water, he was reminded of how little he knew about vehicle repair. As the only guy in the vehicle, he feared his manliness might be called into question.

Kendell was sitting close enough to his side that Cheesecake was able to stretch out over both their laps. "I wonder how many people tried to ride out the storm."

Having to zigzag through neighborhoods to find the

higher and dryer roads made it easy to see which homes had occupants and which had been hastily boarded up.

"They didn't have much notice," he said. "I've always thought that was the one saving grace of a hurricane—enough warning time to get out of town. This one was more like a giant tornado that came out of nowhere and dumped a lake's worth of water on the city."

Minerva made some tight turns to get around debris that had been washed into the street. She stopped the bus and pulled the clackety handbrake. After a moment, Myles realized they were in front of the Scratchy Dog. He'd never before seen Frenchmen Street empty of cars and people.

The club had suffered the usual storm damage: The uneven cement floor had miniature lakes of standing water, the big front window was nothing more than shards of glass, and the bar was covered in bottles—both empty and full—making the place look as though someone had thrown one wild party. Other than the water on the floor, most of the damage looked to have been caused by opportunists thinking the night before might have been their last on Earth. Having raided the Laroque summer home, Myles wasn't going to be judgmental. However, he did hope Charlie had had the good sense to straighten up before the last of their party left.

With everyone pitching in to clean the place, the afternoon felt more like a continuation of the party from the night before than work. Even Cheesecake lent a paw, though only in her normal supervisory position. Sitting on the room's musty couch, she looked like the club's unofficial mascot, and she received far more pats than duties.

With the glass swept up, Myles inspected the loose shards still hanging on the window frame. "We should board this up. I'd hate for someone to get sliced open by one of these."

Polly took a microphone stand and busted out one of the triangular pieces of glass. "No way. Punch them all out. I want the gig tonight to be one big street party."

Myles doubted the modification would be appreciated by the building's owner, but he wasn't around. "I wonder if there's a law against breaking in and rocking out."

"I've always wanted this band to be more edgy," Polly said. "Getting arrested for playing would certainly add to our mystique."

With the heavy work done, Kendell took Myles to one side. She pulled out an expensive bottle of rum he assumed she'd appropriated from the bar. "I need to know what happened to Sanguine. Of course, if you can find out about the cane, Colin, and Baron Samedi, that would be great, but I'm most concerned about Sanguine."

He was still perfecting his ability to be a good boyfriend, but some emotional traumas weren't hard to figure out. "You're afraid she didn't survive the hurricane?"

"That or the fight over the cane. If she's hiding somewhere, I need to know so I can help."

The outdoor courtyard behind the Scratchy Dog hadn't been battered nearly as badly as the club. Metal tables and chairs were still positioned for a quiet conversation or a private affair. Myles set two glasses on a wet table and pulled a couple dry chairs from under the balcony.

Papa Ghede materialized as Myles poured the rum. "You've had quite the eventful couple of days."

Myles seldom had someone available to explain the answers to his life's events. "What happened to Colin, Sanguine, and Baron Samedi?"

Papa Ghede drank his rum like a person hoping to forget his past. Myles had seen plenty of such customers at the bar. "I don't know."

"Bullshit. You know everything that happens among the living and the dead."

The dark voodoo loa's eyes sparkled like black diamonds. "The challenge of knowing everything is to survive the boredom. I noticed people find meaning in learning about other people. As I know everything that every person is up to, that sense of mystery wasn't really possible for me. But as no one was telling me what to do, I changed the equation."

Myles wasn't looking for more metaphysical nonsense. He just wanted to know if Sanguine was okay and if Colin Malveaux was still a threat. "All I'm asking is who ended up with the walking stick."

But apparently Papa Ghede wasn't content with such trivialities. "I'm trying to explain to you *why* I don't know. A certain amount of mystery between people helps them bond together. Getting to know one another is key to the relationship's growth. But since I knew everything about everyone, I was denied that fundamental part of life."

"So you changed the equation?" Myles began to understand. "You're talking about the voodoo loas."

"Exactly. But not just them. To truly have other beings to

relate to, I divided up some of my powers and offered them to the recently deceased. You understand I couldn't trust such power to the living."

"Of course. Even a little power, and we end up with a baron Malveaux."

Papa Ghede smiled over his glass of rum. "That's how the voodoo loas came into being. But you're among the living. Not everyone believes the same thing about existence."

"So you created other religions, too?"

He helped himself to another drink. "What people believe is like a multifaceted diamond with the truth at its core. People are free to peer into whichever window they like, but each is separate from the others as a test to see if a person has seen the truth or is too enamored with their particular perspective." Though Myles enjoyed a lively conversation about the nature of existence, Papa Ghede could get a little overly philosophical when he drank.

"I still don't see how that prevents you from knowing what happened to Colin and Sanguine. Are they still alive?"

He seemed to have been more interested in the drink than the question. "What a person believes becomes their reality. Take you, for instance."

"Wait a minute. Just because you're sitting here doesn't mean that I believe in voodoo."

"No, of course not," Papa Ghede said. "Had you followed the practices of voodoo, you'd be no more than a disciple. You believed in the *deep waters*. That made you an equal to the loas of the dead."

Myles wasn't sure he liked where Papa Ghede was

headed. "Sanguine didn't believe in voodoo. Her perspective was Wicca. Where does that leave her in your world?"

"Herein lies the problem. When she tossed the walking stick into the tempest, she moved it from the realm of voodoo to that of Wicca. Colin Malveaux dove in after it, thus removing himself from my sight as well. The cane's transfer cast a shadow over those who were involved. They are not in the *deep waters*. Guinee is a land of unknowns for me. It's my place of discovery. Colin and Baron Samedi might be there, but I have reason to believe they aren't."

Myles hated that Papa Ghede kept so many secrets about Guinee. "Why don't you think they're there?"

He gave Myles a long, hard look. "I suppose, as a permanent visitor to Guinee, you have a right to know. Not all of the loas get along with each other."

Myles remembered his time getting to know each of the loas of the dead. "I did notice that Baron Kriminel and Ghede Nibo weren't on speaking terms."

"You are very perceptive. After Kriminel killed Nibo, Baron Samedi took in Nibo in the afterlife. This made Kriminel and Samedi enemies."

Myles had never been clear on how, exactly, Archibald Malveaux had come to possess Baron Samedi's cane. "Did Baron Kriminel tell Malveaux how to steal the staff?"

"You're beginning to understand the situation. So long as the baron Malveaux had the walking stick, he held Baron Samedi's power. This worked in favor of Baron Kriminel. Power struggles aren't limited to the living."

The idea that Sanguine had somehow created a new form of hell was looking more likely to Myles. "So if they're not in Guinee and not among the living, that only leaves the realm of the witches."

Papa Ghede frowned at the empty bottle. "I have more questions than answers about that possibility. The witches have their own intermediary plane between the living and the dead. Ultimately, we all end up in the *deep waters*. I find it unlikely they would welcome Colin Malveaux into their purgatory if he was holding Baron Samedi's cane. It's also not a place he'd go willingly as he's a practitioner of voodoo."

Myles began to see why the power of the hurricane had been necessary. "So they forced him into a realm they created."

The old voodoo loa's eyes turned as black as endless voids. "Creating a new afterlife is no simple matter. If a soul is pushed into it, there has to be a gate from life to the new death. Obviously, that gate must be guarded. Then the realm itself must have rules, and that involves rulers to keep the status quo. Assuming the voodoo cane got sucked into that new reality, that would create another gate—this one between this new afterlife and Guinee."

Myles didn't need to be told of the potential results of a spirit passing through a gate without acceptance from both sides. "And with every gate, there exists the possibility of conflict between the two sides. Such a new reality doesn't sound like something a beginning swamp witch could create within a few days."

"There are many questions. The disappearance of Baron Samedi is very disquieting. He is already a gatekeeper in Guinee. Were he to find himself in this new afterlife—

trapped with his adversary—he might take it on as his personal mission to be the new gatekeeper or, possibly, the ruler."

Myles grew suspicious of Papa Ghede's intent on being present. "Something tells me you're not here just to answer my questions."

The old man's smile did nothing to lighten Myles's apprehension. "You straddle many realities. Baron Samedi belongs in Guinee as guardian of the seventh gate. If he's missing, we have a rift between the living and the dead—one I will have to fill as his substitute until he returns. And if Colin Malveaux has the cane in the realm of the witches, there could be a war between voodoo and Wicca. We have too many doors and not enough watchers."

How did you gods ever get along without me?

BY FIVE IN THE AFTERNOON, the club's floor was dry enough to no longer be a safety hazard. The place still smelled musty, but that beat the aroma of garbage steeped in drainage water, which permeated most of the neighborhood.

The generator out back made enough of a racket to be heard on stage, but Kendell didn't mind. Frenchmen Street was typically pretty noisy most nights, anyway. The band would easily drown out the small motor with their playing.

Myles's report about the afterlife struck panic deep in her soul. She still didn't know what had happened to Sanguine. Transferring her frustration onto him, simply because he couldn't find the answer, wouldn't be fair. His reasoning that the new swamp witch couldn't have created the afterlife did nothing for her anxiety. Obviously, Sanguine was the only one with the answers, and no one was out looking for her—not that Kendell had any idea of where to start.

She tuned her electric guitar, hoping the gig would distract her from her worries. Cheesecake was safe, back in the apartment, and Myles would stay at the club, working as a fill-in bartender with Charlie. His and Cheesecake's safety were the most important things. She wished her pooch was fonder of the band's playing, but noisy, large crowds made the old girl nervous.

Professor Yates had sweated through his T-shirt, trying to electrify the club. "There is enough power for your instruments but not much else. I'm afraid it's going to be warm beer and candlelight tonight."

Polly wore her typical short black skirt over ripped fishnet stockings, which looked normal and helped combat Kendell's feelings of unease. "So long as they can hear us in the street. Word of mouth is going to be our only advertisement tonight."

Charlie had been busy organizing the bar. "I've got a few concoctions up my sleeve for when there's no power. There might not be much in the way of variety, but I suspect people will be more into alcohol content than taste. Storms have a way of simplifying the palate."

Polly had always maintained a keen awareness of every band member. She nudged Kendell as she looked over the makeshift operation. "Lighten up. You look like a drowned puppy. We're supposed to be helping the community feel like getting back to normal."

Kendell knew she was right, as the club was one of the few establishments able to reopen so quickly. "This is a good thing we're doing. I suspect a lot of people would like to either get out of town or hole up with their depression."

The bandleader gave Kendell's guitar case a light kick with her high-heeled stiletto. "If you've got that golden pick in there, this might be a good night to let it rip. We could all use a dose of your high-octane energy."

Kendell pulled it from her pocket. "I've been keeping it close."

"Good. We'll only have a couple of hours before the city's curfew kicks in. Let's make it a post-hurricane party to remember. No songs about storms, just loud, in-your-face music. You do your best Joan Jett. People love it when you go all dark and intense."

"Only if you pull out your inner Debbie Harry."

People had been milling around the club all afternoon, so when Polly stepped up to the microphone, she didn't have to work too hard to gather their attention. "We've only got one measly generator tonight, so we're going to need you all to make some noise!"

A polite smattering of cheers went up from the sidewalk.

"You're not getting it. Sing along, sure, but go get your instruments—drums, horns, empty five-gallon buckets, whatever you've got. Don't leave us poor girls up here all alone." Her coquettish innocence didn't fool anyone.

With Charlie and Myles manning the bar and the band at their usual positions on stage, Professor Yates forced open the water-swollen door to let the loiterers know the club was open. "No cover and free drinks. All we ask is you tip what you feel you can afford. This is New Orleans, and we are all in this together."

Polly stomped out the opening beat to "One Way or Another." The crowd was into the song even before Minerva had a chance to add in the drums.

Kendell got lost in the music, as always. She could feel the crowd electrifying her with their energy, and she, in turn, gave all she had to create the perfect vibrations with her strings. More people gathered with each song, and as they expressed their love of the music in whatever way they could, she experienced all they'd been through. They'd spent their day slogging through the wreckage that had been their homes and lives just a few days before. The release of hearing music gave them something to grab hold of, and she embraced them right back.

Music was her mystical power. She took their pain and filled the void with optimism. The people were alive. They'd weathered the storm. All they needed was to understand the power that gave each of them and how much they could do together.

Other musicians joined in across the street, which had filled with people—the guys from Cutting Heads and the Mutants from Table Nine, who usually played after Polly Urethane and the Strippers, and so many street musicians that she had trouble telling if they were a group or individual performers.

As the band poured everything they had into "I Love Rock and Roll," Kendell saw a clearing in the crowd. In the middle was a beautiful woman, spinning so quickly that her vintage ivory lace dress flew around her like waves on the ocean and her long blond hair wrapped around her face. As the song ended, the woman faced Kendell and pointed at her in acknowledgment.

Kendell's heart felt about to explode as she returned the gesture to Sanguine.

16

*B*ack in her apartment, Kendell held Sanguine so tightly that she thought her arms might give out. "What the hell happened? I was so worried about you."

The woman's long blond hair, which Kendell had only seen soaked in sweat and swamp water, now cascaded in soft, vanilla-scented waves around her face.

"The plan worked," she answered.

Kendell's irritation threatened to replace her feeling of relief. "You have to do better than that. Where's Colin Malveaux, Baron Samedi, the fucking cane? I'm not some tourist gawker asking out of curiosity. I need to know." She let go of Sanguine and sat next to Cheesecake and Myles for the long-awaited answer.

"Now that my grandmother's life's work is complete, I guess I can tell you. Agnes Delarosa wasn't your run-of-the-mill swamp witch. Her mother, my great-grandmother, was the one who Marie Laveau originally trusted as curse guardian. Agnes was born to watch over the Malveaux curse. With Baron Malveaux in Guinee and all of his cursed possessions well hidden, that meant, for over a hundred years, her primary duty was to sit and watch. But she was also an oracle. She knew what was coming. She had mad skills as a witch, and she had nothing but time. Do you really think *I* was the one to invent Colin's hell?"

Though Kendell knew the living side of voodoo, Myles was more versed in what actually went on in Guinee. Fortunately, he didn't sound as suspicious and hostile as he did with Delphine. "Your grandmother built the hell, and you forced Colin into it?"

"I didn't force anything. He could have stopped chasing after the cane. My grandmother knew he'd become the 'rabid dog' as she called him. Not everything was clear to her. Oracles often see patterns more than actual events. She'd hoped Lincoln Laroque would change his ways, but in case he didn't, she wanted to make sure she'd be the first to know his plans. Baron Samedi's cane was like a meaty bone she waved in front of him to see how he'd react."

Kendell could tell Sanguine was stalling. "I'm well aware of the Laroque family's obsession with power. And no one understands Baron Malveaux better than Myles. What we need to understand is what cage your grandmother built to contain Colin."

Sanguine rolled her eyes like a high-school girl trying to talk her way out of detention. "That's what I'm trying to explain to you. There's no version of hell in Wicca. Even voodoo only has Guinee, which isn't really sufficient at holding someone prisoner. Answer me this. What's the opposite of the *deep waters?*"

Kendell turned to Myles, who'd spent far more of his life studying the subject.

"The *deep waters* are the sum total of all human souls," he said. "It's the universal connection we all experience in life but can't define. So I guess the opposite would be complete isolation."

"Exactly. Agnes referred to Colin as the family's fulfillment. What she meant was all of the Laroque's ambition had been bred into Lincoln. Those physical traits that were painstakingly cultivated by intermarrying members of the family—and only bringing in outside partners if they added to the gene pool—was only the outward manifestation of their goal. The family elders distilled all the greed and lust for power into Lincoln. Then, when he ingested the baron himself, Agnes knew her life's calling had reached its end. Imagine all that greed taken out of the *deep waters.* Her work was to improve humanity by cutting out the cancer."

Myles took his time responding, which told Kendell he too saw Sanguine as a younger sister who'd done her best. "I can see the allure of doing something that seemed like an ultimate good. Such actions don't come along often. I guess, in her shoes, I might have spent my life trying to remove some greed from the human experience as well, even if it only amounted to a small modicum of that vice. Our worry —and this comes from the loas of the dead—is what's holding him in your grandmother's creation? Does he have Baron Samedi's cane? Because if he does, your grandmother is up against a far more powerful adversary than she thinks. And what happened to Baron Samedi? Is he also in this new version of hell? If Colin Malveaux were to break out of this prison—either into Guinee or what we know of as life—we may be facing a devil we can't control."

Sanguine stamped her foot. "You know, you can be a real buzzkill."

~

COLIN CAME to on the side of a gravel road. The hard-driving rain mixed with the blood running from the cuts on his face and arms and dyed the swamp water a deep brown. Attracted by the scent, crawfish swarmed around him and pinched voraciously at every piece of exposed skin.

He was still alive. The realization created an insane, hysterical laugh that he struggled to control. From the lack of hurricane-force winds, he knew the storm had passed. However, the black clouds continued to cover the sky so thoroughly he couldn't guess if it was day or night.

The pragmatist in him argued he needed to assess his strengths. The sheets of rain made it hard to see. Off in the distance, his once-pristine SUV was wheels up in the swamp. It took him longer to spot Delphine's old Cadillac, which Sanguine had stolen, at the end of the road. He'd have missed it, but as it was hanging precariously fifty feet up in a tree, it made the limbs creak and crack with every sigh of wind.

Sanguine was nowhere to be seen. He found comfort in the fact she wasn't towering over him with her look of artificial superiority. With any luck, the wind that had taken the Caddy had also whisked her far out into the bayou.

He needed to get up and find out what had happened. Those answers weren't to be found by lying at the side of the road. Every muscle hurt as he rolled over and attempted to push himself up off the ground. The effort set his side ablaze. *Cracked ribs.*

He fell onto his back and performed a more careful assessment of his body's condition. He could move his arms and hands. They were bloody but functional. Next, he tried bending his knees. Though his left leg performed as expected, his right leg remained in the swamp, where the crawfish were rushing to resume their meal. The rain was noticeably darker as it ran into his right eye. He touched the gash in his forehead, trying to measure its length and depth. He needed something to stop the bleeding.

Despite his privileged upbringing, Colin had learned the basic first-aid skills any kid born in the South had been taught from earliest childhood. He stripped off his once-elegant coat, now torn to shreds, and his silk shirt, which hadn't fared any better. Finally, he tore his cotton T-shirt to ribbons and bandaged his head and arms. Making a splint for his leg took a little more ingenuity, but the edge of the bayou was full of driftwood swept down from the Mississippi.

After an hour of wallowing around in the mud, he made another attempt at standing. His ribs still burned so badly that he found it hard to breathe, but otherwise his medical skills seemed sufficient for him to save himself from the mudbugs.

Flashes of lightning over Lake Pontchartrain backlit the New Orleans skyline. Not a single building had power, but at least he knew where he was headed. He estimated the Quarter to be twenty miles away, but with any luck he'd run across someone willing to help within a mile or two. People had a way of riding out the storm rather than risk losing what little they had to looters. Wheel ruts in the gravel were filled with water, but not a car was to be seen. *Stay here and die, or get walking.* He took one last look around the scene of destruction, seeing no cane, no Baron Samedi, not even the evil old swamp witch who thought she'd won. If that was her version of hell, it looked an awful lot like the reality he remembered.

With each step, he felt his confidence returning. Sanguine had failed. The old swamp witch had failed. Even Baron Samedi had failed. Colin might not have the cane, but he had his life. As long as he existed, he could fight his way back. Battered and bruised was not the way to leave an adversary, especially one with so much power. All they'd managed to do was piss him off.

By the time he found the main road, he was itching for a fight. The pain in his leg and ribs only added to his rage. He looked both ways down the deserted highway, searching for some sign of life he could exploit. The only movement was the continual driving rain. *No matter. The closer I get to the Quarter, the more cowering people will be longing for a leader.* Despite his injuries, he no longer needed help. As always, he would take what he wanted.

As he approached the town of Gretna, he wondered if everyone had finally grown brains and left when they'd gotten the order to evacuate. Not a single car was on the freeway. He listened intently for any buzz of a home generator. All he heard was the continuous storm.

The day had been incredibly long. He needed to get out of the weather, attend to his bandages, and get something to eat. If the neighborhoods really were empty, then each house was fair game. The first street he turned down looked as if the residents had prepared for a zombie apocalypse. The houses weren't just boarded up—they'd been covered in welded metal sheeting. *What the hell were you people expecting?* The next street was no better. He shook his head at the residents' paranoia. Even after Katrina, the small bedroom community had turned its back on New Orleans's refugees. He couldn't expect much better of people while a storm was still raging.

He returned to the freeway and braced himself for walking the whole way to New Orleans. *I've made it this far.* Even from the small suburb, he could see his penthouse looming from atop the highest skyscraper in the city. With each burst of lightning, he raised his head and felt his office beckoning him home. *Fuck 'em all.*

A nagging thought finally took hold of him as he approached the Crescent City Connection, which crossed the Mississippi River. He hadn't found evidence of a single person. It seemed beyond improbable that every man, woman, and child had run from the storm. He started looking for evidence that anyone was still manning the infrastructure that kept the city going. Not a single light shone in any window of any building. In cases of power outages, some buildings always had their own generators.

He stared over the edge of the bridge. Ships needed attending to, even in the worst weather. Not only were there no longshoremen, no ships were there, either.

Panic was not an emotion he'd ever accepted. No matter how long the odds were, he always found a way of turning the tables on those who would defeat him. *I must get to my office. From there, I can figure out a plan.* Dogged determination had served him well in the past. All he had to do was hold fast to one course of action. He dragged his splinted leg with renewed vigor.

His anger grew when he hobbled off the freeway and onto the city streets. He looked up and yelled at the storm, "I'm not buying it! You hear me? There are always cars on the streets. No way every vehicle gets out of town. Your simulation sucks, so you can just knock it off right now."

He knew he was talking to himself. Even if the old swamp witch was getting even with him for bonding with Baron Malveaux, she wasn't about to answer him. *My vengeance is going to be swift and merciless.* Now that he knew the game, the time had come to start planning his moves.

BOOK LIST

Technopia Series:
(writing as Greg Chase)
Creation
Evolution
Damnation
Salvation

The Malveaux Curse Mysteries :
(writing as G.A. Chase)
Dog Days of Voodoo
You, Me, and the Voodoo Queen
Oops! I Voodooed Again
Voodoo You Love (coming soon)

Other Stories
Through the Lens

ABOUT THE AUTHOR

G.A. Chase is the pen name for Greg Chase. He is a science fiction and paranormal author living in New Orleans with his wife, fellow author Deanna Chase, and their two shih tzu dogs. On any given day you can find him behind his computer, people watching in the quarter, or out in his studio creating stories in glass. His glass work can be found at www.chase-designs.com.

www.GregChaseAuthor.com